I0564193

THE WRONG MAN

THE WRONG MAN

Christine D. LeBlanc

IGUANA

Copyright © 2021 Christine D. LeBlanc
Published by Iguana Books
720 Bathurst Street, Suite 303
Toronto, ON M5S 2R4

All rights reserved. No part of this publication may be
reproduced, stored in a retrieval system or transmitted, in any
form or by any means, electronic, mechanical, recording or
otherwise (except brief passages for purposes of review) without
the prior permission of the author.

Publisher: Meghan Behse
Editor: Alison Larabie Chase
Cover design: Donald Lanouette, Ottawa Brands
Author photo: Flash Designs Studio

ISBN 978-1-77180-540-7 (paperback)
ISBN 978-1-77180-541-4 (epub)

This is an original print edition of *The Wrong Man*.

To Stephanie Benning Figueroa, Tracey Ellison and Ian Brannen,
who never had the chance to read it themselves.

AUTHOR'S INVITATION

The main event at the centre of our story really happened. Well, in a way. I invite you to see if you can deduct fact from fiction. See you at the end.

CHAPTER ONE

The man of Macy Carruthers's dreams looked up from the dead body and waved, awkwardly.

Well, actually, she wasn't sure he was the man of her dreams, but she had decided to at least learn his name. Today was the day she was going to introduce herself to the stranger she had been noticing regularly over the last couple of months. Now she was having second thoughts.

Five minutes earlier, she'd had a bounce in her step as she strode through the lobby of the nursing home. Her strawberry blonde hair brushed her shoulders as she walked, and her motorcycle boots made her taller than her usual five feet. Because it was Sunday, and it was always special to visit Vaughn, she had added a nice blouse, the same shade of medium blue as her eyes, to balance her riding jeans. As she waited for the painfully slow elevator, she transferred her leather jacket to her right arm, balanced her helmet with her left and looked around. It had taken only a few visits to memorize all the notices and signs around the lobby, so she looked to the small table beside the chairs instead. The newspapers in the waiting area were old: The front page had a headline about a drug bust that had happened a couple weeks earlier. She remembered it being splashed all over the news, with several prominent local businessmen caught up in the sting, along with members of a family suspected of having mob ties. Finally the elevator arrived and she stepped on, hitting the button for the fourth floor.

For months now she had been arriving as an attractive blond man with a muscular build was leaving with a much older man, presumably his grandfather or some relation. It had happened so often they had gradually started nodding, then saying hello. If he hadn't been hot enough to make her hormones set off bells and whistles in her head, she wouldn't have noticed him at all, not in her just-out-of-a-bad-breakup state. But she figured she was about one bad relationship away from owning too many cats, and so she had decided the time had come to initiate contact with the opposite sex again. Today she was going to make the bold move of learning his name. Baby steps, for practice if nothing else. Not that she'd turn something down, but she didn't want to get ahead of herself. Just his name, to start. Maybe that would erase the brain itch she had whenever she thought about how odd it was they kept crossing paths, him leaving just as she was arriving.

That was before she reached her destination and found the handsome stranger standing over an obviously dead person. It was enough to give a girl some serious doubts.

The body was that of an elderly white man, face down, the white hair covering his head matted with blood.

Without thinking, Macy stepped forward. An arm shot out from beside the doorway to prevent her coming any further into the room. On a taller person it would have struck the chest; on her it was nearly a blow to the face. "Sorry, miss," a young uniformed police officer said. "This is a crime scene. You can't come in."

"But he's here!" She pointed at her stranger, who spoke up. "I found him."

"Is it..." Macy looked at the body again, not wanting to say the words.

"Macy!" Whirling about at the sound of her name, she saw her old family friend coming towards her down the corridor, an orderly at his side. She breathed for the first time since seeing the body.

"Vaughn!" she exclaimed, throwing her arms around him. "You're safe." She inhaled deeply, breathing in the mix of pipe smoke and aftershave from his gray cardigan. He was thin — too thin, she thought. His crop of white hair was sparse across the top, and the veins showed particularly blue today in the white hands that held her. But she had known him her whole life and rarely noticed how elderly he had become. He was just Vaughn, always there.

The tall man patted her back tenderly. "Ah, there, there. I'm fine. More than I can say about Victor, though."

Macy pulled back to look at him but didn't let go. "That's Victor? Oh, Vaughn, I'm so sorry. What happened to your roommate?"

"Ms. Carruthers," another voice called down the corridor. Gordon Bruin, the manager, strode up to them and shook her hand. Macy was Vaughn's main contact, so the staff at the nursing home knew her well. Bruin was usually onsite only during regular work hours; he must have been called in for the emergency. Instead of his usual suit, he wore khaki slacks and a navy blue golf shirt that strained against his paunch.

"It seems as though Victor fell and hit his head. We think it was an accident, but the authorities have to be sure. That means Vaughn cannot return to his room, and unfortunately we don't have a spare room at the moment; we're full."

"Alright." Macy digested this bit of news for a second. "Vaughn, would you like to come stay with me for a few days?" Mentally, she was already rearranging her small apartment to accommodate a guest.

Vaughn waved her off. "Macy, you don't have room."

"I'll take the couch. It'll be fine."

"No, no, don't make a fuss. I don't want to put you out. You do enough already."

The old man was visibly upset. She thought fast, afraid to upset him further by arguing. She didn't want to suggest a hotel, where he'd be alone all day. He and Victor had been roommates for a while now, and their friendship had been good for both of them. Macy wanted to comfort Vaughn somehow, make sure he wasn't alone just after a friend's death, especially one that happened so close to him. And he had to go somewhere. But if he wouldn't stay with her... That left only one solution she could think of.

"Hey, you know what? What about Derek's? He'd love to have you. And think of Anabelle."

Vaughn brightened at the mention of the little girl's name. "Well, maybe for a couple of days."

Macy smiled at him. "Okay then, I'll just give Amy a call. I'll be right back." She turned to Bruin and asked to use his office. He nodded and gestured back down the corridor. She walked there alone as Bruin stayed with Vaughn and the police. As soon as she turned away, the smile fell off her face.

Clinging desperately to the hope she could minimize actual contact or think of a better solution in the next few seconds, Macy reached the office, entered and pulled her cell phone from her jacket pocket. The word "misgivings" crossed her mind and made her chuckle at the understatement. But it was for Vaughn. He needed her to step up and suck it up.

She took a moment, leaning against the desk, staring at the phone. Finally, taking a deep breath, she hit the digits for Amy and waited. Her friend answered on the third ring.

"Hi Amy, it's me. Um, bit of a situation here. Do you have a minute?"

Macy explained what had happened with Vaughn and asked if he could stay at the house. A few minutes later she disconnected the call. As she expected, Amy had instantly agreed, and both of them knew Derek wouldn't need to be asked.

Macy took advantage of the quiet office to take a deep breath before leaving the room. She looked around and saw signs of Bruin's personality: a candy dish full of jelly beans, a couple of framed photos of people she assumed were his wife and children. Family. Macy had known Vaughn her whole life, and he needed help. She wasn't going to let him down, no matter what it cost her. She'd just have to suck it up. In many ways, he had been a grandfather to her; sometimes more of a guardian angel. She felt bad even hesitating and thinking of herself. *Really, how bad could it be*, she thought, and the knot in her stomach clenched its reply.

She returned to the corridor and found Vaughn sitting in a chair by the nurses' station across from his room. The manager was speaking with the police, and the handsome stranger was sitting with her old friend. They both looked up as she approached.

Macy smiled at Vaughn. "Amy's on her way." She put a hand on his shoulder. "Are you sure you don't want to keep me company?"

He chuckled and patted her hand. "You work too hard as it is. I'm not disturbing you. Besides, you're in an apartment! Where would I smoke?" He used his other hand to pat his shirt pocket, where his ever-present pipe lived. While not allowed to smoke inside the nursing home, Vaughn did enjoy his strolls outside for fresh air.

The tall blond stranger stood and extended his hand to her. Well, he was actually of average height, but everybody was taller than Macy.

"I'm Thomas."

"Macy. Pleased to meet you."

"Likewise." They shook. He gave her a real handshake, not too hard, but not mushy either.

From this close, she could see the fine lines at the corners of his vivid blue eyes that turned down a little at the edges. His warm smile animated his face. Creases in his brow made him seem more masculine and a bit weathered, a nice change from the pretty boys and hipsters she was used to. His eyebrows and the slight shadow on his jaw were a darker version of his thick, wavy blond hair. Previous assessments had hinted he was muscular, solidly built. By how much she had to angle her head to look up at him, she estimated he was a smidge under six feet tall. Mentally, she registered that his calm demeanour hadn't changed despite the situation. He smelled good and felt good too.

Movement from inside Vaughn's room startled her, and she realized they were still clasping hands. Macy also suspected she had a silly little smile playing on her face, which was inappropriate considering the circumstances but perfectly natural given his … well, him. She dropped his hand hurriedly and looked away. With his hand still extended, he gestured to the chair beside Vaughn.

"Would you like to sit down?" He offered his chair, which she waved off. He remained standing, leaning against the wall beside the chair, facing her.

"I'm fine, thank you. Was Victor…?"

Vaughn jumped in. "Thomas here is my friend's grandson. Buddy comes to see me, he has a crush on one of the nurses. On Sundays, we play chess, I smoke, he flirts. Thomas drives him back and forth."

"Oh, that must be the gentleman I see you with sometimes," Macy said, before she could consider the implications of admitting she had noticed and remembered.

Thomas nodded. "I'm sorry we're meeting under these circumstances, though." He tipped his head towards the room. Macy nodded, then turned back to Vaughn.

"Actually, Vaughn, if Amy's going to be here soon to take you to Derek's, do you want to pack some things?"

He shuffled to his feet and they approached the room, where Macy asked the uniformed officer if they could gather some of Vaughn's clothing. They got a nod from the cop and in a few minutes had packed an overnight bag, while trying to step around and avoid the body still lying on the ground. When she could, she gave Vaughn's hand a squeeze and patted his back. Soon they were ready to leave, but Bruin pulled them aside in the corridor. He asked if the contact information they had for Macy was correct, then he asked for Amy's phone number as well, for the time Vaughn would be staying with her at Derek's.

"Terrible business, this. I am very sorry about this, Vaughn. We'll get you back here as soon as we can, but it seems the police think it may not have been an accident."

"What?" Macy had heard him fine — she was just shocked.

"Well, Victor did have a visitor just before he was found. Vaughn, you were playing chess in the gardens. The visitor didn't stay long; no one saw him leave, actually, but it's odd enough…" Bruin took the business card Macy handed him with Amy's phone number and the address of her childhood home scribbled hastily on the back. "In any event, the police may have some questions for you, Vaughn. And also for you, mister…?"

"I've already given the police my information," Thomas replied. Bruin thanked him, then Macy asked the manager about Victor's next of kin.

"Would you mind letting us know of any funeral arrangements, once they're made?" Bruin assured her he'd pass her request on to Victor's family, then said goodbye and returned to his office.

As Macy, Vaughn and Thomas turned down the hall towards the elevator, Thomas turned to Macy and reached for Vaughn's bag.

"May I take that for you?"

It took a second for Macy to register the offer, before she handed it to him with a thank you. Their hands touched briefly and he gave a little smile.

"No trouble at all." At one point in her life, when she had more to prove, Macy would've turned down the offer and carried the bag on her own. But dating a few self-centred jerks could teach a girl a thing or two about appreciating simple manners. Well, maybe just one jerk, she thought, but one really big jerk.

They walked past the nameplate next to the room that read *V. Marlow, V. Monroe.* Vaughn was V. Marlow; Victor had been V. Monroe.

"Where's your grandfather now, Thomas?" She made a mental note of the formal name: Thomas, not Tom, not Tommy.

"He left. Too much, ah, it was a bit too much for him, I'm afraid. I stayed to answer some more questions from the police."

"Oh, I hope he's okay."

Thomas gave her another smile. "I'm sure he'll be fine, thanks."

She had to remind herself something horrible had happened and she really shouldn't have noticed how his biceps had bulged under his shirt when he crossed his arms while leaning against the wall, or how his smile made his eyes crinkle at the corners. *Macy, you're a bad person*, she told herself, *and you're going straight to hell.*

They exited the building and had just reached the sidewalk when Amy pulled up, parking her red Ford Focus in front of the doors so Vaughn didn't have far to walk. Thomas quietly handed the bag back to Macy, who smiled and repeated her thanks. When Amy got out of the car, she went straight to Vaughn for a hug, then they put the bag in her trunk, and Macy gave Vaughn another hug before he got into the car. After promises to call back and forth, the car pulled away, and Macy turned to Thomas to say goodbye, but he wasn't there. She did a slow circle to scan around her before she realized he had vanished.

And there he goes again. Rather annoying, that, she thought. *Well, at least I got his name. Mission accomplished.*

As she strode to her bike, she tried not to calculate how many cats would fit in her apartment instead of disappearing men or other houseguests.

August 4, 1950

Dear Diary,

Today's the big day, I'm finally 18! Mama and Papa both say I can leave home now. If I have to get a job, I'm going to the big city! Well, not the big big city — Mama and Papa say New

York City is just too big, they'll only let me go if I stay in nice places, so I'm gonna try Canada. It's close and must be real nice. Maybe Toronto or Montreal. Montreal might be neat, cause it's French and all. It'll be like going to Paris but I can still come home to see everybody. I've been looking forward to this for so long and now it's finally here! I'm sooo excited! I'm packing my suitcase and leaving first thing tomorrow morning. Look out big world!

CHAPTER TWO

Macy Carruthers's name did not appear on the list of tenants in her apartment building's entranceway, and it never would. She walked past it straight to the elevators after work, a few days after Victor's untimely death. From what Amy told her, Vaughn had settled in so nicely, he might never want to return to the nursing home. That would be good for him, bad for her, as then she'd be forced to cross paths with … so much she had tried hard to avoid.

She didn't bother checking her mail, since she did most bill transactions through online banking and hardly anyone else had her address. Her best friend and former work colleague, Ellie, occasionally sent postcards from her travels, but that wasn't regular enough to bother checking.

At various times in her life, she had had a wide circle of friends she could call upon for fun, social activities. For the times she didn't want to be alone. None of them really knew her well, though, except for Ellie, who had gotten closer than most. Macy was still in the making-friends stage at her new office. There was one woman who was a potential friend. She smiled as she thought of Tracey, who sat next to her and who had quietly pushed over a box of cupcakes to share one day. They were starting to talk about common interests like movies and music, but for now Tracey was simply a work acquaintance. Macy wouldn't spook her by opening up about her brother, Derek, yet. Or how she felt about potential contact, now that Vaughn was staying at her childhood home, currently shared by Derek, Amy, Amy's fiancé, Joshua, who was Derek's childhood best friend, and Amy's daughter Anabelle. The thought of going back there put Macy's stomach in knots. Not the type of baggage to share with a colleague.

She rode the elevator to the sixth floor that was really the seventh, but since the building had a ground floor and twelve more above it, some creative re-numbering had been used to avoid the dreaded number thirteen. At the end of the hall she opened her door and, once inside, dropped her overflowing bag in its usual spot. The keys she tossed onto a small side table as she kicked the door shut behind her, then used one hand to lock it.

She kicked off the three-inch walking shoes that brought her up to average height for a woman and stretched as she walked through the living room to the balcony window, the hems of her gray pinstriped pants now dragging a little on the wood floors. She pulled at her button-up cream shirt to untuck it. Macy often stood at the balcony, gazing out. Below her were various shops, while directly across were other apartment buildings, resting atop another layer of stores. So many people, she thought, her eyes scanning windows. So many different stories.

She had been back in Toronto for almost a year now. Her family history hadn't made it easy to find a job in her field, even with her master's degree in criminology and her training as an investigator. Security clearance background checks were a bitch, as her name often came up as a witness or alibi or next of kin in other people's records. Macy also had to admit to being part of the problem. Since graduating, she had refused to come anywhere close to home, and since that meant avoiding the country's largest city, her options were limited considerably.

For a few years she worked in small towns and cities growing with natural resource booms. It was a nice way to see the country, but she really wasn't a small-town girl. Even if she liked a place, she quickly grew restless, and would move on once she had conquered a job's challenges. Eventually she grew tired of doing basically the same job over and over in a new place, again and again. Macy could have made an entire career out of helping to prevent theft and sabotage in the forestry, mining and oil sectors, but there was only so far she could go without either joining a larger company or starting her own.

When the towns and jobs and people started blurring together, she'd finally been ready to let her ambition overtake her stubbornness and decided to get out of her own way. She was lucky to find a small company that was just starting up and willing to take a chance on her, but it meant moving back to her hometown. Macy hadn't spent any significant amount of time there in years. Since her high school graduation, she had gone back only once, for her mother's funeral, and she never looked back.

Pain and guilt rose inside her when she thought of her mother's death. Macy hadn't realized how serious her mother's condition had been until it was too late. Her mom hadn't wanted to bother her, so Derek had been told not to tell her. Not that the siblings were really speaking by that point, anyway. Macy would call her mother weekly but had refused to talk to or about either Derek or her dad.

Macy still thought of her mom every day, missed her, wanted to talk to her. Wished she hadn't been so hard on her when she left town for school. But back then, after what happened at her graduation and in the following weeks, it was all an emotional blur. It seemed to her teenaged self that almost everybody in her life was letting her down all at once, and all Macy wanted to do was put her home in the rear-view mirror.

She was looking back now, though. In all the years she had avoided it, the city had never stopped feeling like home. Toronto was Canada's biggest city with almost three million people now, but most neighbourhoods tended to be self-contained pockets. Growing up, her family had had everything they needed within a ten-block radius, and her mother never even learned to drive. That was in the core, though, in an area that had no other name, close to High Park and the Junction.

Now Macy was in North York, in a one-bedroom condo apartment she had bought during its construction. Yonge Street stretched out below her, with Finch Avenue to one side and Sheppard Avenue to the other. Her area was also somewhat self-contained. She could take the elevator straight down to the underground shopping complex for her groceries and entertainment, or hop on the subway to get around the city when she didn't want to drive. She usually took the subway to work. She had established a favourite coffee shop, where she'd take a book on the weekends to get out of the house, and a few regular restaurants for takeout. She was starting to develop a routine but there was always something new to do, see and try. Macy was enjoying getting to know the city as an adult and often played tourist.

Before moving here, she had wondered if it would be hard to avoid her old stomping grounds; if she'd ever slip into old patterns, old habits. So far she was doing fine. In the big city she revelled in her anonymity, but also knew the Murphy's Law of running into old acquaintances in the least expected places. Would they try to find her, if they knew she had come back? Which would bother her more — them trying, or not trying at all?

Shaking the thoughts from her head, she shoved off from her perch and started walking towards the kitchen. Along the way, she stopped to turn the radio on. Too much time alone, too much silence, was starting to get to her. She missed having someone to do things with, like Ellie. Both Ellie and Amy would go stark raving mad with her lifestyle, and thinking of the two very different women made her smile. Ellie kept herself almost too busy, and Amy did not do well alone without a man.

Macy had about an hour before her exercise class: enough time to eat and digest. Then she had an entire weekend to fill up and no visit with Vaughn at the nursing home to look forward to. Maybe she should give Ellie a call and take some time to chat, rather than their daily texts and weekly emails. That would depend on Ellie being back from one of her many whirlwind work trips, though. Macy would have to check. At the very least, she'd have to update her friend on finally having met the mysterious man at the nursing home. Mysterious, indeed.

A thought of her ex-boyfriend flickered across her mind. Killing time was easier to do when she was dating someone, she thought, thinking of him for the first time in a while.

Vinnie — or Vincent, as he preferred — had filled some gaps for her. Brushing off the random thought and wondering what had made him pop up in her brain, Macy walked towards her bedroom to change her clothes, then stopped suddenly.

The bedroom door was closed.

She never closed it.

Instantly hypervigilant, she listened for sounds in the apartment. When there were none, she glanced at the front door. It had been locked when she came in — she was sure of that. No tampering. Softly, she padded towards the bedroom, grasped the doorknob and, as she swung it open, dropped into a crouch.

Nothing. Staying light on her feet to remain quiet, she entered the room, looking all around, even behind her. Using similar movements, she checked the closet, then under the bed. If anything, the neatness was odd. Usually she was in a rush in the morning, but apparently hadn't been that day.

A little more relaxed, but still wary, she repeated her search in the rest of the apartment. She didn't find anything but had walked by her answering machine a second time before she realized the blinking red light meant someone had called and missed her. *Vincent?* she wondered. Very few people had her phone number. She liked to think she was selective, exclusive even. Not hiding. Her ex was one of the few. Why she was thinking of him now, she didn't know, and she was bothered by it. She could still remember the smell of his cologne, an intimate detail she hoped to forget soon, along with everything else about him.

Cologne! She was remembering his scent. Although she couldn't imagine why. He hadn't been in her apartment since the night they broke up. *And that's enough of that,* she thought, focusing again on the blinking light.

Trying to ignore the leap of excitement she felt — she was going to have to work on getting more human contact — she hit the button on the old machine. It still worked, so she saw no reason to switch to an automated service that would cost her more. Plus, it had been a gift from her father, one she cherished because he had actually purchased it like other people's fathers. It came with a receipt in a bag from a store, not a story about a guy who knew a guy who got a great deal off the back of a truck. Macy stood looking at the red light as a familiar voice came through. Both regret and relief hit her when she realized it wasn't Vincent.

"Macy, it's Vaughn here. I need to, ah, I need some cash. So if you could, just, whatever it is you do to my money, I need it soon, okay? Um, I think, I think ten thousand to start. Maybe more, later. Okay, thanks. Call me when you have it. Soon, please."

Quickly she hit the buttons, rewound the message and played it again, this time listening to the underlying current of stress in his voice. Ten thousand dollars, fast? Maybe more later? What was going on?

When she was growing up, Macy's family never had much in the way of savings, because her mom would use anything she had to try to keep her dad out of jail. Vaughn had come through in a crunch, giving Macy the money for university. The gift changed her life, but she wouldn't be surprised if it wasn't general knowledge. Vaughn was always helping them here and there, doing good in small, quiet ways. She had paid him back, insisting on adding interest, and now handled some of his finances, so to her it was obvious that he'd ask her for help when he needed money. It was her turn to take care of him.

Once more, her gaze turned to the view outside. If her guardian angel was in trouble, she might have to reveal herself sooner than she expected; face her demons. Well, at least her brother. And her past. Sooner than she wanted, and not on her terms.

She wasn't ready.

CHAPTER THREE

Thomas heard it, but in the flurry of activity no one else noticed. He peeked outside and saw a small motorcycle with an equally small rider pull up in front of the house. The bike was black; the rider was in gray and blue. He had seen the bike before, but never with the rider still on it. Intrigued, he leaned against the wall to watch from an angle. After parking, the rider swung a leg over to stand beside the 250cc cruiser, then took off the helmet. Shaking out her hair, she turned to face the house. Thomas leaned back a little to avoid being seen as a smile came to his face. Behind him, the others were starting to sit down at the table: an old man, a woman, a child and two other men about his age. He joined them, awaiting her knock, feeling something close to nervous. He hadn't seen her in this environment before; then again, he hadn't been around the house much, or known the group for very long.

He sat down beside Derek and handed the potatoes across to Joshua, still thinking about that strawberry blonde hair. The shaking out after the helmet removal reminded him of a shampoo commercial. He smiled again. Once there was a break in the "could you pass the" conversation, he asked, "Shouldn't we wait?"

Several forks paused as heads turned to look at him. It was Derek who asked, "For what?"

Thomas gestured towards the front of the house as he turned his head to reply, but a movement in the doorway caught his attention. There she was, the rider, leaning against the doorframe, surveying the dinner scene. The buttons of her jacket were open, her helmet was in her hand and she still had her sunglasses on. Up close, even in her boots, she was small, one of the details he had noticed about her at the nursing home. Activity stopped as everyone turned to look at her. In a low voice meant to carry, she said to Vaughn, sitting at the head of the table: "You called?"

Thomas noticed heads turning from the rider in shock to Vaughn in confusion. It was Anabelle who broke the silence. The ten-year-old jumped from her chair and ran to the rider, shouting, "Auntie Macy! Auntie Macy!"

Macy set her helmet down in time to catch Anabelle and sweep her into her arms. Her smile was instantaneous and the hug was tight. The child was almost as big as she was but she lifted her with ease. "Hi, sugar plum! How are you?"

By then, so many startled glances were flying, Thomas couldn't keep track of them all. Amy followed her daughter in hugging the newcomer. Vaughn pulled a spare chair over to the table and made room beside him, to Thomas's right. Joshua stared at Macy, and Derek stared down at his plate.

"Welcome, welcome! You're just in time for dinner. Come, sit." Vaughn held the chair out for her. Macy hesitated.

"I didn't mean to interrupt. Can we just talk for a minute?"

"Of course! After dinner. Sit, sit, it's getting cold."

"I can't stay, I just wanted to talk to you…"

"Can't, or won't?" Derek finally looked at her. The mood shifted from pleasant to tense. Thomas wondered what that was about.

"Does it matter to you?" she shot back. It was Anabelle who dragged her to the table, not letting go of her hand.

"Stay! You can't go yet, you have to eat before you get a treat."

Macy looked imploringly at Amy, who just shrugged and went into the kitchen for an extra plate and cutlery. Relenting, Macy plunked Anabelle back in her chair beside Amy's, then took the one Vaughn offered.

"Hi, Joshua."

"Good to see ya, Mace."

Macy shrugged off her jacket and hung it on the back of her chair. Finally, she turned to Thomas as she pushed her sunglasses to the top of her head, moving her hair away from her face. She looked at him with big eyes that looked startlingly blue with her reddish hair.

"What are *you* doing here?" She didn't mean to be rude, but she was too shocked to see him knit into the scene to be polite.

"This here's Thomas," Derek said. Evidently he didn't know the nursing home connection. But Macy didn't know any other.

"Hi there." He offered his hand and got a surprised look before she shook it. He murmured, "Nice to see you again."

Still Thomas, not Tom or Tommy? Shaking hands? Different, this one, Macy thought. And he hadn't answered her question, but Derek did.

"He's my friend, Macy. He's welcome here." There was a negativity to his tone, but Macy ignored it, focusing more on her confusion.

"But how do you know..."

"What brings you by, Macy?" Amy interrupted without noticing.

"Vaughn called, it sounded ... important." She glared at the old man, who pretended not to notice.

"I called Friday, you came Sunday, it can wait until after dinner."

But Macy continued, with an accusing tone. "I tried calling you back and you refused to pick up. You wanted to see me in person. Then I couldn't find you at the tavern, at the corner store, in the park or anywhere else."

"Vaughn didn't go outside all weekend," Anabelle piped up. "He didn't even take me to the park."

Vaughn was definitely avoiding Macy's gaze, and now Derek's too. "What's so important ya called *her* for?" Derek asked carefully, lacing the reference to the newcomer with scorn.

Thomas noticed a similarity in the way Derek and Macy were looking at Vaughn, who mumbled, "It can wait until after dinner." Thomas turned to Macy and tried to cut the tension, but his mind went blank and he spit out something obvious.

"So ... is that your bike outside?" He already knew it was but thought it would be a safe topic. He just needed a conversation starter to talk to her. One that didn't involve how he had left without saying goodbye last time. He had realized Amy would recognize him that day at the nursing home, so he'd just quietly slipped away. It wasn't like him to act so strangely; he just didn't want to make the situation worse. Macy had already found him standing over a dead body, and although he had nothing to do with that, aside from being the one to find poor Victor, he didn't think it was the best time to explain his connection to her family. It was complicated enough.

Macy slowly turned her gaze to him, but kept it there only a moment. "Yes." Not yep, not yeah. He noticed she didn't speak or hold herself like the others. Then she focused on the food before her. Joshua picked up the thread.

"Still have the Virago, Mace?" She nodded, spooned a few token pieces of food onto her plate and set the bowls down. She was stiff, her movements a little jerky. She was definitely uncomfortable here. "That's what, at least ten years old now?"

"A new one, actually. Old one finally bit the dust." Joshua got a bit of a smile from her. That meant Derek was the problem, Thomas thought.

"How long are you in town for?" Joshua asked. Macy didn't get a chance to answer before Anabelle did. "You have to stay forever! You have to play with me more!"

Macy smiled at her biggest fan. "I'm going to try, sugar plum honey bunch!"

Derek's fork fell to his plate, maybe dropped, possibly thrown. Macy and Amy exchanged startled looks. Joshua sat back, realizing his attempt to make things better wasn't working.

"Whatchya come back for?" Derek asked, staring at her. She stared back.

"Couldn't get a job anywhere else. Security checks, family history, you know." That last bit was said as a jab. Derek stabbed at his food.

Thomas started putting the pieces together in his mind. This was the prodigal daughter, the sister who had left and didn't come back. Thomas had once seen a picture of the whole family in a frame on the mantel. It was his sister's high school graduation, Derek had said, before giving the photograph a funny glance and walking away. Then one day, to Thomas's surprise, he ran into her at the nursing home. He was too startled at recognizing her from the photograph to say anything. He'd thought he would have met her by now. Then, as time went on, it became a little awkward, as he tried to figure out how to get an introduction without coming across as a stalker or, at the very least, a weirdo.

He recalled the first time he and Derek had met, in a jail cell where they were being held overnight on separate charges. Shortly before pot was made legal, Thomas had gone to pick up his younger sister at a house party, arriving just as the police raided it. He claimed her pot as his own and had spent the night in custody, until the family lawyer convinced the police to drop the charges. It was his first encounter with the system. Derek had been brought in on suspicion of breaking and entering, but he was let go the next day as well. He had been in the wrong place at the wrong time and was rounded up with the usual suspects. During the long night in the cell, they struck up an unlikely friendship, even more so considering Thomas's privileged upbringing and Derek's blue-collar one. But Derek himself didn't realize how different they were, since Thomas always played down his background.

That night, though, to pass the time, they had talked about almost everything, including family. Thomas told Derek of his wild, spoiled younger sister who thought she was ready for anything and whom he adored. Derek spoke of his smart, hard-working younger sister, who was the first in the family to go to university, with near-reverence, so clear was his pride, some affection and a touch of sibling rivalry. Thomas couldn't reconcile the defensive brother and sister before him with the image he had formed that first night. He had expected them to be as close as he was with his own siblings.

But, come to think of it, no one else talked about Macy either, although apparently she kept in touch with Amy and Anabelle here, and Vaughn at the nursing home. That graduation photo was the only one of her in the house, the only one showing the whole family, and Thomas knew because he had been spending quite a bit of time there lately. Looks-wise, she hadn't changed much from that photo, in cap and gown, parents beside her and Derek with his arm over her shoulders. By the tension in the room, Thomas imagined the siblings' hands would be around each other's necks instead now, if they were given the opportunity.

This time Macy herself broke the silence. "So, how are you settling in, Vaughn? And when did you all start eating together?" She turned to Thomas. "All of you." She gave him a rather pointed look. It was just too much coincidence, finding him here, she thought.

"One big happy family," Derek muttered. Amy jumped in.

"Vaughn suggested we start eating dinner together. It's good."

"Huh." Macy looked between Thomas and Vaughn again, then between Thomas and Derek, trying to figure out the connections.

Thomas continued to check her out surreptitiously. Blue jeans, which made sense for riding a motorcycle, but a fashionable top, not low-cut or too tight; something that would fit in anywhere. Almost anywhere. Thomas chuckled as he thought of how he dressed down himself, "slumming" as his stepmother would say. But even his slumming clothes were more expensive than the ones this crowd usually wore. Macy wore less makeup than Amy, and he thought he could smell a nice fragrance. He noted the small studs she wore, three in each ear. In the length of time it took him to count them, she noticed he was looking at her. He quickly turned his head and asked another question. "So where do you work?"

"I'm a security consultant." She answered politely but avoided giving a company name. Joshua snickered and Amy hit him.

"What? Oh c'mon, it's funny. One of us…"

"She's not one of us," Derek pointed out.

"She's all mine!" Anabelle said. "She's my friend!" Macy laughed softly, then winked at the little girl. "You bet, sugah!"

Finally the meal was done, and Macy joined Amy in the kitchen to clear away the dishes.

"You've done an amazing job keeping quiet about me, Amy," Macy said quietly with admiration as she grabbed a dish towel and stood by the counter.

"Was afraid you'd hightail it outta town again," Amy said, shrugging. "Besides, you should be thanking Anabelle. She's been bursting to see you again." She paused for a moment. "Derek asks about you sometimes, you know. Like you ask about him sometimes. It's been really hard keeping my mouth shut, girl!"

Macy chuckled and wiped down a dish, placing it in the right spot in the right cupboard automatically. That unnerved her for a moment. So far, so good, she hadn't melted. But if she didn't get out soon, her stomach would be in a knot permanently. It was too strange to be there in the kitchen without her mom, without… She almost grabbed the next plate from Amy in her hurry to be done.

"Sorry. Ah, so how's Vaughn doing? Still upset about his friend dying?"

Another of Amy's shrugs. "He said he didn't want to be at the home anymore, that he needed somewhere else to live, a new place. We said he could stay here for as long as he needs to. He helps out with Anabelle, you know. He watches her sometimes and takes her to the park so me and Joshua can have some time together."

Oh yes, her high school sweetheart was now living with her best friend. *How times change*, Macy thought. "So, all of you in this house, that cozy?"

"Well, everyone but Thomas. He's a new friend of Derek's. Don't know where he lives, come to think of it. Anyways, Vaughn took the room down here, in front. Joshua and me have the big bedroom upstairs. Anabelle's next to us, in your old room. Your brother is in the basement now; he's done it up real nice. It made sense to save money, till me and Joshua can get a place of our own."

"So what's his deal? Thomas, I mean."

Amy stopped and looked at her. "Why, you interested?" A big smile splashed across her face.

Macy rolled her eyes at her friend. "He was at the nursing home too. Just before you showed up. He brings his grandfather to visit Vaughn sometimes. Apparently they're old friends, or something."

"He does?"

Macy nodded. "It's just too weird, that he's there and he's here too."

"Maybe it's fate."

That elicited a groan from Macy. "C'mon. You don't think it's odd?"

Amy shrugged. "The world's a lot smaller than you think, you know. Seriously, maybe you were meant to meet him."

Macy realized her stranger-danger brain wouldn't be able to communicate with Amy's hopeless romantic one on this topic and, sighing, she gave up. They moved on to the glasses and cutlery. "Speaking of men, any word from…"

Amy knew where she was going and finished her sentence. "From Anabelle's biological daddy? More like sperm donor, he was gone in such a flash. No, nothing. Not at birthdays, not at Christmas. But Joshua, he's doing real good now. Steady job, and he's a daddy to her." Amy's soft brown eyes met Macy's blue ones. "Things are good now, Mace. Not like they used to be. The boys are grown up. They haven't been in trouble in a long time."

Macy busied herself with putting dishes away. Amy was trying to convince her it was safe to be there. But she knew better. If she let her guard down, she'd be trampled again. And she had so much more to lose this time. She had come so far, but it was so fragile.

Amy filled the momentary silence as she wiped down the counter and stove. "Aren't you gonna ask about…"

"Nope. Because I don't care." With a flick of the towel Macy was done. She pulled Amy into a quick hug. "It's always good to see you, though."

"You too, Mace." Amy smiled as they pulled away, and together they walked into the living room, where the others were waiting.

Vaughn was sitting in the worn armchair that had always been his usual spot, for as long as Macy could remember. There was a yellow stain on the ceiling right over top, where his pipe smoke lingered. Once, when Macy was young, she'd asked him why he smoked a pipe instead of cigarettes like everyone else. "Gets the girls," he'd said. That was his response to most questions about why he did things. Yet Macy could never remember him with a girlfriend, and certainly not a wife. In fact, the only women she ever recalled seeing him with were her grandmother, then her mother, then herself, and now Anabelle, who was examining the late-day whiskers on his chin. They were having a very frank discussion about why his hair was white and hers was brown.

Macy again leaned against the doorframe, not wanting to extend her stay. Derek picked up on it and said snidely, "We don't wanna keep you from something important."

"You couldn't," was Macy's instant retort.

Derek, too, was leaning, against the window on the far side of the room. Amy sat beside Joshua on the couch, and Thomas took the other chair. He wasn't sure what was going on, but he wasn't going to miss it.

"Vaughn, let's talk." She used her authoritative voice and jerked her head to indicate they should leave the room. It startled Vaughn out of his conversation. Amy plucked Anabelle up and left, talking to her daughter about playing in her room for a while before bedtime. Anabelle protested all the way up the stairs.

"Okay, so talk."

Macy shot him a look of incredulity. "First of all, you sure you want to talk in front of everyone, and secondly, you called me!"

"So I did, so I did. And I don't see why we can't talk with everyone, we're all family."

"What about him?" Macy nodded her head towards Thomas, who sat up under her notice. He was feeling a little miffed she wanted to exclude him,   especially now that something was finally starting.

"He's cool. Met him in jail, actually. He's more part of us than you are," Derek threw in from across the room.

"Jail. You met him in jail. Figures." Well, there went that idea of chatting up the hot guy at the nursing home. Who was now in her home. Well, her old home, and that was just too weird. She sure could pick them. Macy tried to shrug it off, but couldn't resist another comment. "Don't you find your criteria a little odd for making friends? No offense, Joshua."

"Forget about it." Joshua and Derek had been friends since grade school. They had all grown up together, playing, then hanging out, then getting into trouble. Macy was the only one of the group who had left the area. It made her an outsider, and it made them feel left behind. Her good grades gave her the ability and her ambition gave her the will to leave. Through her, they saw what they couldn't have, and they resented it, believing her choices to be a judgment on their own lives.

Thomas felt stung that Derek had thrown out the fact that he had been in jail so easily, and more so that Macy had dismissed him. A stint in jail, even just overnight, gave him credibility with Derek and Joshua, but took it away with Macy. He knew Derek and Joshua both had records, but technically he didn't. Sure, he would do it again to protect his sister, but that wasn't the point. For some reason, he wanted Macy to think he was different, better than that, although he had spent his time here trying to fit in. *Figures*, he thought, *you're going to blow it with a girl.* And a snobby one at that. Again, he chuckled internally. He had never been on this end of snobbery before. But somehow he wanted to impress her, when he really shouldn't stand out.

Of course, she didn't know that and couldn't know why he was chuckling again. *Oh, that's right,* she thought sarcastically, *everything's changed. Derek's still hanging out in jails and bringing strays home.* And she was still attracted to the wrong people. At least she found out early this time, before she got any closer. The life of a crazy cat lady was beginning to have some appeal, despite Thomas's sparkling eyes, laugh lines and nice build. She quickly looked away from him. She could learn to like cats.

"Look, Vaughn, can we just get down to business? What's going on?"

"Why don't you start, Mace?" Joshua suggested.

"Alright. Vaughn called me on Friday, said he needed money. What for?"

"Since when?" Derek called.

"Since when what?"

"Since when does he call you for money? He got us, don't need you."

"You still pick up friends in jail and it's *his* judgment you're questioning?"

"Alright, alright, you two, enough," Vaughn said from his chair, gesturing surrender. "Derek, Macy here, well, she handles some things for me."

"Like what?"

"How is that relevant?" Macy countered. She took a deep breath and tried not to revert to her mouthy younger self with her brother again.

She continued, trying to speak to him in a measured tone. "On Friday he called and said he needed cash, a lot of it, fast. So the question is either, what's wrong with you, Vaughn, or…" She turned to Derek again. "Or what have you done now?"

"I ain't done nothing!" Derek took a step towards her. She stood up and faced him straight on. *So much for maturity*, she thought.

From where he sat, Thomas was in the middle. He looked from one to the other, alarmed by the sudden escalation and amused at how similar the siblings were. Derek's hair was more brown but still had a reddish tinge. He was more angular than Macy, but it was clear they were related. They even took the same stance, feet wide with hands on hips, confronting each other. Somehow Thomas doubted they'd appreciate any mention of it, though. They were bookends of righteous indignation, one large, one small.

Vaughn finally spoke up. "Settle down, you two. You're so eager to pick up where you left off, you don't see what's changed. There's no need for this. We need to work together." After a moment both Macy and Derek stood down and went back to their separate leaning positions across the room. Thomas felt as though the bell had sounded and they were retreating to their corners of the boxing ring.

"Now," Vaughn said. "Alright, alright already. There's a bit of a problem."

Thomas watched Macy's reaction carefully. There was definitely concern there, overriding her earlier annoyance. "Start at the beginning, Vaughn," she instructed him, coming to sit on the couch's arm so she could lean on the armchair and towards the elderly man.

"Oh, the beginning is too long ago. Suffice to say, I did some things that, it seems, haven't been forgotten." He dug into his pants pocket and pulled out his wallet. "But, ah, your grandfather was involved too." He handed her a piece of paper.

Macy scanned it quickly, then looked at him in shock. "This is a blackmail letter!"

"What?" Joshua shuffled on the couch and leaned over Macy's shoulder to see the letter. Even Derek stepped forward, but stopped himself before he came too close to his sister.

"So it would seem."

"It's dated a week ago. You got this at the nursing home?"

Vaughn nodded. "He knows too much, probably about your grandfather too. And he followed me here. Friday, I got another. Delivered here." He stressed his point as he handed her a second note.

The first said, "I know what you did with the priest, 1950. If you don't pay, everyone will know, even the police. Instructions to follow."

The second read, "First instalment of $10K. Drop off next Friday. Instructions to follow."

They were computer documents, printed on plain paper. There was nothing distinctive about them aside from the meaning behind the words. Macy read them out loud. By the second note, Derek was hovering even closer, and Thomas was peering over her other shoulder.

"He's testing to see if you can pay," he commented.

Aftershave? Macy inhaled again. Yes, it was aftershave, a nice subtle one, and it was on Thomas, who was very close. He returned her gaze until she looked away again. *What kind of criminal wears good aftershave?* Warning bells went off in her head. *The smart kind, the kind who makes money*, she thought. *The slick kind.* She could see there were flecks of green mixed in with the blue in his eyes. His wavy blond hair was trimmed short. *That's irrelevant, Macy*, she thought, forcing herself to look away again. *Focus!* Still, he didn't seem to fit... *Neither do you*, she reminded herself. She then had to remind herself not to lean towards him.

"If you do come up with the ten grand, he'll hit you up for more. It won't stop." Thomas spoke, startling her a little.

Her curiosity about how Thomas was so familiar with blackmail was overridden by her concern for Vaughn.

"How bad would it be if it came out?" she said softly, handing the notes to Joshua, who handed them to Derek to read. She moved forward to take the older man's hands in hers and spoke softly.

"Vaughn, what happened? What did you do?"

CHAPTER FOUR

Everyone turned to stare at the old man, who fiddled with his pipe, uncomfortable under their scrutiny. Derek took the notes back to his window, Joshua slid back on the couch, allowing Macy to take Amy's place, and Thomas took her place on the arm of the chair.

"It's a long story, so long ago."

"We need to know. What would the police do if they found out? What's the worst case scenario here?" Macy kept her voice low, authoritative and comforting, not shrill or alarming.

Vaughn took a deep pull on the pipe, let out a couple smoke rings, then settled back in his chair. "We were younger than you all. Things were different back then, you know. It was the start of the 1950s. After the war, things were good. There was opportunity. Population was booming, between all the babies and immigrants. The DPs, displaced persons, after the war. Women went back home when the men came back to their jobs. Then all the babies came," he said with a chuckle.

"You didn't need university or college — hell, you barely needed high school. Only thing we had to worry about was commies, the Communists, the Pinko Ruskies. The Cold War blew up right here in Canada, did you know that? Up in Ottawa, where I grew up. Gouzenko was his name, Igor Gouzenko. Russian clerk stole papers that showed spies here in North America. That was the start, before the Americans went crazy about it." He sighed before continuing.

"Pearson at the UN, our troops helping in Korea, Suez Canal. Things were looking up for Canada, for everybody. To make sure it'd last and we didn't get another bloody Depression, we got the old age pension, other social services. And now look…"

Macy interrupted gently to get him back on track. She usually loved these history chats, but they needed to get to the point. "Vaughn, blackmail. Please focus."

He shifted in his seat, took another breath. "I grew up on a small farm outside of Ottawa. Quebec is right across the river, like Windsor and Detroit down here. Ottawa's two hours from Montreal, four from here. The border with the States wasn't that far away, just over at Cornwall. Your grandmother, Libby, was born in the States. You never knew that, I don't think. She grew up in a small town just on the other side. Bobby, your grandfather, he was my cousin. He lived close to me and my family. He'd come stay in the summers, work on the farm. Us and the chickens. When we were young men, not much more than teenagers really, we got into this and that for some quick cash. We wanted off the farm so bad. We wanted to be somebodies, you know. Any chance we got we hightailed it to the city."

"Ottawa," he said, pointing his pipe in her direction, "was a hotbed of activity. It was the bingo capital of North America." He nodded and paused.

Macy realized she had been on the edge of her seat and leaned back. "Bingo?"

Vaughn nodded again, not recognizing the disbelief in her voice. "Bingo," he repeated. He was obviously the most, if not the only, impressed person in the room. Thomas pitched in.

"Wait — Montreal had the French Connection and Ottawa had — bingo?"

Macy's face lit up in a smile as she recognized another history buff, until she remembered they were discussing the terribly serious issue of blackmail. In her family. And Thomas was a wild card, or at least an unknown, no matter how good he smelled. She got back to business, but not before he noticed she had perked up for a moment.

"Vaughn, what does this have to do with the blackmail notes?"

He rolled his eyes. "Tell me something. Would a million bucks impress you?"

"Ah, sure."

"Well, imagine that — sixty years ago! That's what the bingo pots were going for! It was big business, I tell ya. It was the kind of gambling churchgoing folk could feel good about. The charities all ran it. They gave away cars, lots of cars, every night. Back then it cost two hundred bucks to buy a television, two grand to buy a car. They were giving away so much and made even more! Thousands of people would come to town — they ran buses in from all over! It was the scene, I tell ya."

"And then?" Macy prompted.

"Then." Vaughn took a puff. "Then the mob came to town. They followed the money."

Amy returned to the room and everyone resettled, letting this new information sink in. Vaughn continued.

"Ah, there was a good side. Kids were getting milk in school, hospitals were getting new equipment. But all that cash… They had so much they needed Brinks trucks to haul it all away every night. That caught the attention of the mob. They came up from Montreal. Started running scams, to start. Forging cards and planting a caller so they'd always win. But that was just small time, getting their foot in the door. They moved up and started moving in on the charities.

"You mentioned the French Connection, eh?" Vaughn used his pipe to gesture towards Thomas. "Heroin from Turkey shipping out from Marseilles in France, stopping in Montreal before ending up in New York. You think that's when it all started? Hell, the mob's been in Montreal forever.

"We weren't thinking about the mob though, or anybody else. We didn't know what was going on in the bigger picture. We was just kids! Young punks. We saw all the money flowing and wanted to be part of it. We thought we were going to get rich, all in one summer. Bingo was the biggest racket in town, and no one could say anything bad about it, 'cause all the best people were involved. Bobby had a buddy from Montreal who could get us into the racket, show us the rounds. The guy got into it when the car dealerships started competing for the charity business. He'd drive the new cars to town for the different bingos. That's how big it was! Companies falling over themselves to get a piece. We started finding cars all over, mainly Montreal but going into the States, bringing them back up and selling them to the charities to give away as prizes. Didn't even need a passport back then! It seemed so glamorous, so grown-up. Then I met a girl, and I wanted to show off."

Vaughn relaxed somewhat and smiled at the memory. He took a long drag off his pipe and held it, holding onto the picture in his mind at the same time.

"It always starts with a girl. Ah, she was sweet. Met her just outside of a small town in New York State. She was hitching, trying to get to Toronto or Montreal. New York City was too big, but her hometown was just too small. I made your grandfather pull over. That was different too, hitchhiking. Even a nice young girl could do it without thinking and be safe. Still remember her hair in the sun." His voice got soft and he looked down at the pipe in his hand for a moment.

"She held so tight to that suitcase. Introduced herself proper and thanked us for the ride. Think she was nervous and excited, all at once. We got to talking for the rest of the ride. By that time we were also picking up liquor for the bingos, other prizes, whatever we thought they'd take or what they asked for. Our first stop was a bar that was giving us booze cheap. I took her inside, trying to impress her with how sophisticated I was, how badass I was, and wouldn't you know it, the cops show up, and there she is, underage and sticking out like a sore thumb. Had to be twenty-one back then, not just nineteen. Us fellas got out 'cause we were loading the truck by the back door, but she was lost in the crowd and ended up on a paddy wagon.

"I felt bad. I couldn't just leave her in the clink like that, her being new in town and not knowing anybody and all. We went to the police station and stood outside, trying to figure out what to do, then there she was, coming down the steps. Seems a priest had been in the bar too, and they got to talking as we made our delivery. She was telling him we were there to help the charities. She didn't know he was our contact. That's why he was there. He took a shine to her. He convinced the cops to let her go.

"We should've grabbed her and run, but she was a nice girl. She was so grateful she wanted to thank him personally.

Small-town manners. Well, I was sweet on her, so I convinced Bobby and his buddy to wait just a little while more. We found the priest leaving the cop shop later that night. Well, the priest was walking towards a taxi a few blocks away. She hops out of the truck and goes running to catch him. He spots her, starts walking towards us. Just then, a guy comes out of the alley and shoots the priest."

Vaughn imitated a gun with his hand and startled them with a loud, "Pow pow, two shots to the chest. Just like that." They were all sitting on the edge of their seats. The old man paused, frowning at the memory.

Macy waited a moment before prompting. "He shot a priest? What happened next?"

"I jumped out of the truck to get her and Bobby revved the engine. His buddy was riding in the back, and he stood up. Of course, that meant we got a lot of attention from the guy with the gun. He started coming towards us. I grabbed her and pulled her back. The guy started shooting at us. I shoved her into the truck and Bobby tried to swerve around the guy, but he stood in the street and kept shooting at us. Bobby ducked, we all ducked, and wham! We ran him over. Bobby ran him over. He didn't look back, but his buddy told us later the guy wasn't moving when we left him.

"Well, we did take off then. Didn't stop till we dropped off Bobby's buddy in Montreal. Then we went back to the farm, all of us. We brought the girl. I couldn't leave her alone in Montreal. Somehow, she became part of us, we were all in it together, you know. We stayed outta town, we laid low. Didn't tell my folks nothing except the girl needed work and a place to stay. They never found the priest's body, by the way, and not the cab neither. They figured the priest had been kidnapped or something. Seems he had been kicking up a fuss, resisting the mob moving in and strong-arming the charities. The cab driver was the only other witness, the only one who could tell we didn't do nothing. A few months later, Bobby's buddy shows up at the door, saying our names are going around the streets in Montreal. Seems the mob didn't like us on their turf, so they spread it around that we were responsible.

"You gotta understand, back then, the cops, the mob, the whole system was a bit screwy. Not as crooked as Prohibition, mind you, just not all above board all the time. There was none of this prisoners' rights crap. If we got scooped up, who was gonna listen to us? We all waited for it to blow over. Problem was, it never really did. The priest disappearing was like an early Jimmy Hoffa; everybody had a theory. The girl, she didn't deserve it. I wanted to give her a better life. We got word the cops were getting closer, wanted to talk to us about the dead guy and the missing priest and cabbie. We got out then. Even Bobby's buddy from Montreal lit out. We all came here, to the big city. It was Toronto the Good back then. Pretty square, but big. Big enough to get lost in, anyway. Very English, so anybody from Montreal would stick out and we'd notice. Then, you know, time passes. We got on with our lives. The heat died down after a while. But not everyone forgot."

Vaughn paused and swallowed. It had obviously taken effort for him to tell them. Macy gave him a moment then asked, "What happened to the girl?"

Vaughn pointed his pipe at her with emphasis. "The girl was Libby, your grandmother. She married Bobby, the man who killed for her. Your grandfather never got the thrill outta his system, always wanting a piece of the action, even when he had a good life. Maybe in his head he was running from killing that guy. He wasn't the same after, none of us were. You know the rest from there. So here we are."

A moment went by in which no one said anything. Then Joshua asked, "What happened to the buddy?"

"Eh? Huh? Ah, I don't know. Can barely remember his name," Vaughn muttered. Thomas looked at him a bit longer than the others, long enough to catch his eye. Vaughn nodded slightly, then shifted in his seat.

"If you were the one sweet on her, why did she marry Bobby, not you? I mean, you're the one who pulled her into the truck."

Macy always asked the hard questions. He started fiddling with his pipe again. "He did the actual killing for her, to get her, hell — to get us all out of there. Guess it don't get more romantic than that. Small-town-girl manners with a big, bad boy."

For a few moments Macy stared at him. Yes, there was a trace of bitterness in his voice. His answer came too quickly. He had obviously thought long and hard about it himself. His story explained a lot: his dedication to the family, the strong links between him and her grandparents. He swallowed hard. "I got her into it, but he got her out."

"You know any of this?" Derek asked Macy, who shook her head no. "Me neither."

"No one's heard of it. Your father hasn't heard about it and he doesn't need to. It's ancient history," Vaughn explained. "This is the first time I've told the whole story." Macy reached over and held his hand. After a few quiet moments, another question occurred to her.

"Vaughn, does this have anything to do with what happened to Victor at the nursing home? Was that when you got the first note?" Macy's tone suggested she'd take no nonsense. Vaughn just looked at her, a worried expression coming over his face, followed by sadness. Amy filled in the blanks.

"Actually, Mace, the cops say it weren't no accident. He was killed."

"What?"

"Yeah, they called here the other day, wanting to talk to Vaughn some more. Said there was evidence of foul play."

"Oh, no." The seriousness of the situation sank in and Macy took a deep breath.

"Well." She stood and started walking around the living room, thinking out loud. "You can't go to the police about the notes, because there's no statute of limitations on murder, and most witnesses would be gone by now, so all they'd have is whatever evidence the blackmailer has. But you don't have enough money to shut him up for long. And there's no way to know he won't turn you in after he milks you dry anyway. Or worse. Plus, he knows where you live, and that's not good."

Everyone watched her pace. In a few moments she stopped, looked up and announced the plan.

"So, we have to find him, get whatever evidence he has against you and turn the tables."

In her mind she added, *before someone else gets hurt.*

"Vaughn, can you think of what evidence the blackmailer might have?" The old man paused to think, then slowly shook his head.

Thomas noticed how no one thought it was unusual that Macy seemed to be running things. Not even Derek was questioning her authority. He sat back to enjoy the view as she moved about. It was a heavy topic, but it was a nice view.

Suddenly she whirled. "Joshua, you work at an electronics shop, right?" He nodded, adding, "Yeah, two blocks over on Dupont. Saunders Shop."

"You'll have access to the good stuff, and we can get it fast. Derek—" The hostility between the siblings seemed to lessen somewhat momentarily, until they both realized it. They looked away and Macy kept moving, muttering, "Well, you have various skills."

"I work at a garage, thanks for asking." Despite his snide tone, Macy let it go. She already knew, from her check-ins with Amy, but didn't want to let on. Frankly, she was surprised he had managed to hold down a job, but she bit her tongue on that one.

She stopped in front of Thomas. "What are you good for?" *Besides disappearing and reappearing in strange and unexpected places*, she thought. Her hands were on her hips and she gazed down at him, attitude rolling off her. He couldn't tell if she was irritated with him, herself or the entire situation. He expected her booted foot to start tapping. Several answers, most of them sexual, came to mind, but he pushed them aside. Not a good time to be a smartass and definitely not for flirting, no matter how tempted he was.

He looked up at her, not that high, then smiled. "Consider me your bankroll."

One of her eyebrows went up — just one. "Will that cause us more problems later on?"

Vaughn waved her down. "He's a good boy, Macy."

"We can trust him." That from Derek. Still Macy stared at Thomas and he smiled back.

"Based on what? Your bonding in jail?" She tossed that over her shoulder at her brother without looking, still sizing up the new guy.

Vaughn came up behind her, put his hands on her shoulders. "Let it go, Macy. He's okay."

She leaned back and patted his hand, even as she gave Thomas a scowl.

It was Thomas's turn to raise an eyebrow. He let a bit of gloating creep into his smile. She turned on her heel and continued her route. "Fine. So we have to be prepared for another note, with delivery instructions. We can assume it's a guy, most crimes... Well. He'll probably get a stranger to drop it off, but we should watch the house from outside..."

"How do you know that?" Derek wasn't questioning her authority, just her knowledge.

"Pay attention, Derek. What do you think I do for a living? Security consultant, hello? As I was saying, we should hook up some surveillance from in here, and be ready to follow, either on foot or in a car. We have up to four days to cover, and we need to be ready now."

"There's also the money he's expecting," Thomas reminded her. "We'll need to give him a little, tell him we need more time to get the rest."

"I'll have to liquidate some stuff... How much do you think we need?" She was testing him. She already had a plan, and they both knew it.

Thomas considered for a moment. "Three thousand, maybe four. Not quite half, that's too pat. Don't touch any of Vaughn's assets. I'll get the money."

Macy started to protest until Vaughn shushed her again. Assets? What, he's into white-collar crime? That would explain the bankroll, and probably how he knew the blackmail routine. She had to get out of there.

"I'll be in touch." Instead of heading towards the door though, she turned abruptly on her heel and strode to the stairs, calling, "Anabelle, I'm leaving, sweetie. Come say bye." She started up the stairs to meet the little girl partway.

The crew in the living room dispersed, but Thomas waited until Macy came back downstairs. She collected her jacket from the dining room and hugged Vaughn before going out the door, calling goodbye to Amy but not taking the time to find Joshua or Derek. Thomas started to say bye with a wave but she walked right by him without any acknowledgement. Not the reaction he had hoped for. He sat there until he could hear the rev of her engine as the motorcycle drove away.

This was going to be more interesting than he had expected. Of his two brothers and one sister, he was the closest to his grandparents, especially his grandfather. Because he was the third son, he tended to have more flexible time than his older brothers, who both had major responsibilities with the family business already. His younger sister was finishing university and doing the rich-kid travelling lifestyle between semesters. Having heard Vaughn's story tonight, it didn't take much to fill in the blanks — his grandfather was Bobby's friend, the link to the Montreal connections. The rumours about the origins of the family fortune were true, after all.

While Grandfather had seemed amused when Thomas told him of his one night in jail — certainly more amused than his father and stepmother — he had obviously remembered details like Derek's last name. Shortly after that, he had asked Thomas to escort him to visit an old friend of his at a nursing home. Vaughn. Then Grandfather had told him to look up his jail-cell friend, be ready to help with a little matter should it arise, and keep it quiet. He still remembered the words: "Keep your mouth shut and your ears open; now pass the scotch." It was an odd request, but not that unusual; Grandfather always had something going on that he didn't want the rest of the family to know about. Thomas was his usual collaborator. As a result, he had also learned a lot about scotch over the years.

Now Thomas understood the situation, at least a little more. He hadn't made the connection between Derek and Vaughn until the day at the nursing home when he met Macy and heard her talk about Derek, Amy and Anabelle. He still wasn't sure what arrangement there was between Grandfather and Vaughn, but there obviously was one. Vaughn never openly mentioned his old friend in front of the others, and tonight he had deliberately emphasized that Thomas's grandfather was Bobby's friend, probably to divert attention away from the gentleman who visited him at the nursing home. Obviously, Vaughn was trying to protect Thomas's family from being drawn into another blackmail scheme.

I'd like to find out what the deal is with her, he thought, looking at the mantel holding the only picture of Macy in the house. So far, they had only met twice in person officially: once over a dead body, then again over blackmail notes. Things could only get better. He hoped.

August 5, 1950

Dear Diary,

Well I did it. This morning I left and started hitching. At first it was people from home who picked me up and took me a little ways, but then a different car pulled up. A really nice guy hopped out and asked if I'd like a lift. His name is Vaughn and he's from Canada and he's really cute! He's going to Ottawa but says he can take me to Montreal after. He's with his cousin Bobby and a friend named John. They're all really nice. John is riding in the back so I can sit up front with Vaughn and Bobby. We stopped for lunch and Vaughn bought me a cheese sandwich and a lemonade. He said I should save as much of my money as I can for the city. We'll be there soon, and Vaughn says he'll take me out to see the sights. I don't even miss home yet, not one bit.

CHAPTER FIVE

Memories played like a movie reel in her mind. Riding up to the house had been jarring, and she had found her way there more on the deeply ingrained memory of home than by using landmarks. Now, as she drove away, Macy took a little more time to look around.

The houses on the block were built in the 1920s and one side had been completely torn down, replaced by a row of skinnier, stacked townhouses. They were so new the for-sale sign was still on the model home. The row her family house was part of had been spruced up. The wear and tear that had been there in her childhood was no longer visible. A couple of the neighbouring houses that had once been bungalows now had second stories on them, changing the landscape of the block. People were obviously taking care of their properties, or maybe new people had moved in and renovated.

Her house itself looked as though it had had a facelift. It was a brick semi-detached, joined on its left side to an identical house. A front yard with grass and a flower bed lay parallel to the walkway. As she had walked up to the front door she had actually checked the number; the veranda looked that new, no longer showing the signs of neglect that had set in when her family was distracted by bigger issues than home maintenance. The wooden stairs that had been rotting through were gone, and she stepped over solid ones instead. She and Derek had turned it into a game when they were little, she recalled, jumping the third step every time to avoid the weakest board. The dividing wall between the house and the one to which it was attached had been painted over, obliterating her childhood graffiti. The torn mesh on the screen door had been replaced and the mailbox even lacked rust.

The lawn, she noted, was nicely trimmed and mowed, and the plants in the flower bed were doing well. A sure sign of middle class, Macy thought, caring about your lawn. Showing house pride. She had to leave home to learn how to be middle class, and while she was away, home had somehow figured it out too.

As a child she had been oblivious to her neighbourhood's place in the city, but now the gentrification was apparent. She supposed she should have expected it; the area was very close to High Park, and downtown Toronto land values had skyrocketed over the past few years. The very place she couldn't wait to escape now had people in frenzied bidding wars trying to get in.

Sam's Tavern, her father's home away from home, was now a gastro bistro. The Burger Inn, where the teenagers would hang out, had been replaced by a chain restaurant. Macy had fond memories of playing music from small jukeboxes attached to the wall in every booth, and she wondered if there were any chance they were still there. She smiled as she thought of all the quarters Vaughn had given her when she was a little girl. Maybe she'd take Anabelle.

As she rode past what used to be a variety store run by a Greek man named Ben who would squeeze her cheek, and was now a coffee shop advertising the latté flavour of the month, she thought more about her new situation. Macy took a deep breath and let it out slowly. She had gone back and had survived. Derek hadn't seemed thrilled, but everyone else was fine with it. She'd have to see how this played out before making any promises, to Anabelle or anyone else.

Briefly a thought of Thomas flitted across her mind and she tried to bat it away. What he was doing there, what he was doing at the nursing home, why he disappeared... Ah, wait. He'd disappeared when Amy arrived. For some reason he didn't want Amy to see him. She would have connected him to Derek. Hmm. She pondered a little more, but mainly just thought about all the times she had noticed him at the nursing home. To think, just a few days ago she was hoping to learn his name. Now he was learning about her family's criminal history.

That brought her mind back to Vaughn and his story, and to what she had learned about her grandparents. Macy knew what her own mother had been doing when she was her age — dealing with two young kids and a husband who was in and out of jail. Now she wondered what her grandmother had been doing at the same age. She looked around again.

If the neighbourhood had changed that much in the years she'd been away, Macy wondered what it had looked like back in the 1950s, when all this had started. She chuckled as the landscape in her mind took on a sepia tone, then black and white. Suddenly the fashions changed, rotating backwards through all the decade stereotypes like shorthand. The grunge of her university years brightened into the fluorescent colours of her 1980s youth, which faded into the paisleys and corduroy her parents had worn in the 1970s. She could only imagine the 1960s and 1950s. She tried to remember her grandparents, but they had both died when she was very young and she hadn't talked to her father about them very much.

Wait — didn't Tracey live nearby? That fact popped into her head suddenly. She was almost out of the neighbourhood when she pulled the bike over in a parking lot. Pulling out her mobile, she had an idea. Make a friend while checking up on a ... friend? Whatever Thomas was. Or whatever he could be. Nope, she wasn't going there — right? It'd be a good excuse anyway. She wouldn't even have to tell her work acquaintance and potential new friend what else was going on.

Bingo and blackmail, of all things. Murder, mayhem and mystery. She certainly hadn't seen this coming. *Ah, there's no place like home*, she thought as her thumbs typed away.

CHAPTER SIX

Two days later Amy brought in the mail after dropping Anabelle off at school. In between bills and flyers was a plain white envelope with Vaughn's name, nothing else. When she handed it to him where he sat at the kitchen table having his tea, he knew it was the promised instructions. Regret and sadness washed over him as he looked down at it. After all this time, that such a thing would come back to haunt people not even born at the time, it was such a shame. A damn shame. Sighing, he opened it, then reached for the phone.

Macy got the message when she checked her machine from work at lunch. She headed over to the house immediately. By the time she got there, the others were already assembled, all but Amy who, as a waitress, had a different schedule.

Derek was in mechanic's overalls, Joshua was in jeans and a golf shirt emblazoned with his employer's name, Thomas was in dress pants and a collared button-down shirt. He looked as out of place as she did in her dress pants, matching jacket and blouse. Macy spoke to him first.

"Where do you work?"

"Labson's. Big meeting at head office today." He tried to throw her off a bit. There was a big meeting at head office, but he wasn't part of it today. He really did work at Labson's, since it was the family company, but he usually wore a suit.

"A brewery. Great." Macy's eyebrow went up and he thought her impression of him went down another notch. That was not what he had intended. He was aiming for fitting in, not standing out — particularly out of her league.

"We do a lot more than that, you know…" But she was already ignoring him and reaching for the latest note. He was dressed in business casual, not the work jeans she expected if he had the same sort of job Joshua and Derek did. She wondered what his role was; he probably worked in the office, not the plant. She shook her head slightly and tried to focus on the task at hand.

"What did we see on the monitors?"

Joshua spoke up. "Got a plate number. He parked a few houses down, so we caught it on the angle. Looks like a silver or gray car, hard to tell in black and white, but it's an RX-8."

"What?" Her head snapped up. "Give me the plate. I'll run it with our sources at work."

"And where is that?" Thomas tried to sneak it past, but again she ignored him.

"Okay, so he wants a drop on Friday night at … this address is downtown."

"Park or something, ain't it?" Derek didn't get down to the financial district often.

Macy and Thomas both nodded. She turned to him. "Do you have the money?" He nodded again. "Yes, thirty-four hundred dollars, in fifties and twenties, with a few tens thrown in to make it look good."

"Right. He didn't mention what kind of bills he wanted. Bring it Friday and we'll package it for delivery. Joshua, can you show me the video?"

They moved into the living room, where the camera that had gotten the best view was hooked up to the television. With a few clicks, Joshua had the video playing. It showed a man coming up the stairs towards the front door with something in his hand. He turned and walked back down the stairs, then walked to his car, everything clearly visible on the screen.

Quietly, Macy asked Joshua to play it again, then ordered him to freeze it when the man's face was clear.

"Damn," she muttered softly. Thomas was the one who asked her what was wrong, but all three men noticed how she had paled.

"I know him. His name is Vinnie — well, he goes by Vincent, usually. He works in a building across from the delivery site."

"How do you know him?" Derek asked. "Where you'd meet a guy like that?" The surprise in his voice at Macy's association registered with Thomas, although no one else seemed to pick up on the underlying tone.

She stood and faced him. "It's not what you think. He's a financial advisor in the district."

"Then what is he pulling this for?" Joshua looked as confused as the rest of them.

"I don't know. I don't know how he'd find out about what happened when I didn't know myself."

"So how well do you know this guy?"

Macy turned back to her brother. "I dated him for a while."

"You what?" Derek always did have a problem with his kid sister dating. Joshua was the only boyfriend he approved of, and now she had gone and brought a blackmailer home, so to speak. This was not good. She knew Derek was just shocked, but she couldn't ignore the feeling that she had disappointed him. Which was ridiculous, so she let herself be distracted into becoming defensive.

"Don't worry. He broke up with me when he found out where I come from." She walked back into the kitchen.

Thomas was surprised again, this time both by how Macy didn't say it as a jab, just a statement of fact, and Derek didn't argue or question what the statement meant. It seemed to be understood and accepted. He was what he was, and that was how his sister saw him: as something to be ashamed of, something that would hold her back.

In the kitchen, Macy had a glass of water in one hand and was rubbing her forehead with the other. She leaned against the kitchen sink. The others took their chairs again in the living room. Only Amy knew what Vincent had meant to her and what had happened. The broken engagement after he'd run a surprise background check. *Who does that anyway?* she thought. Who runs a background check on a fiancée, then calls off the wedding? The old hurt flamed up inside her. It was subdued but still there, feeding her fear of never escaping her old life, of never being good enough. And here she was, right back in the thick of things... *You can run but you can't hide*, she thought, taking a big swig of water and wishing it were something stronger. *Well, maybe you've learned something from it*, she thought. The melody from The Who's song "Won't Get Fooled Again" started playing in her head.

"But, Mace, you ... you ain't been around here in years. And you don't got a record yourself. Didn't you tell him that?"

She chuckled as she walked back into the living room. She tried to ignore the obvious fact that her brother was on her side for the first time in years, but it came out in her response, softer than it could've been. "It doesn't matter, Derek. It wasn't serious, and it wasn't going anywhere."

"You can do better, Macy." Joshua's voice was soft and kind.

"Gee, that sounds familiar." Macy winked at him. "Thanks guys, but really, it's not important." She took a sip of water, then placed the glass on the table beside her as she perched on the arm of the chair again. As she started talking again, her feet swung in the air.

"But here's the thing. I didn't tell him much about myself at all. We only went out a few times. He was pretty serious, pretty fast, and he has these grand plans to get into politics. He found out about the family when he had someone do a background check on me. Then he broke it off because he didn't want to be associated with someone who had my family history. He thought it might hurt his chances later on or something."

"He just lost my vote." Thomas said it first, but Derek and Joshua nodded agreement.

Caught off-guard by the kind comment, Macy seemed to remember suddenly that Thomas, a practical stranger, was in the room. She looked at him a moment, considered him. He sat there, his wavy blond hair just about to flop over his forehead, his eyes with the crinkles at the corners. So far he seemed grounded, smart. His blue shirt brought out the blue in his eyes. *Remember Vincent*, she told herself. *He seemed like a good thing too.*

Suddenly she was back to business. "So. Even if we confront him, we still don't know how to stop him from leaking what he has on Vaughn. We can prove he's blackmailing, which would get him into trouble, but if we go to the cops the info still comes out."

Thomas picked up the thread instantly. "So we keep an eye on him, string him along, until we get our hands on what proof he has, if any. If we destroy that, he has nothing."

"We go along with the drop, we have Vaughn write a note saying he's working on getting the rest. While Vincent is picking up the money, we get into his place and start monitoring it. Joshua...?"

Joshua was already nodding. "Cameras, phone bugs, his computer ... how much do you want?"

"We don't know how much time we have, so do it all if you can."

Thomas asked, "You have all that?"

"You'd be amazed at how common this stuff is these days," Joshua replied. "Any office supply store has software to monitor emails on employee computers. Every electronics shop sells switches to record phone conversations, and motion-sensitive cameras."

"What can I do?" Derek asked.

"Right now, you can hand me my purse. Then on Friday night you can hook a GPS tracker up to his car, which he'll have to leave somewhere to walk into the park to get the money." Macy was now digging through her purse and came up with a notepad and pen. Scribbling something, she said, "Getting into his office will be harder, but we'll worry about that once we see how much we can get on him at his place, to start."

She tore off a sheet of paper and handed it to Joshua. "Here's where he lives and where he works. We'll need at least two cars on Friday night. One to get Vaughn to the drop-off and have Derek get to his car. The other goes to his house. You and I can do that, Joshua. You," she looked at Thomas but didn't bother with his name, "can follow your money and go with Vaughn and Derek. Unless you're more of a hands-off guy."

"Oh no. I'm definitely hands-on, myself." He sent her a slow smile to underscore the message, hoping she'd pick up on it, but she cut it off by raising her eyebrow. Then she addressed all three men.

"Okay. We have a plan. Any questions?" When no one had any, she said she had to get back to work and left.

Again she brushed by Thomas, but this time he followed her. "Ah, Macy?" He wasn't completely sure what he was going to say next, but he was surprised when she stopped abruptly and whirled around to face him.

"What?"

"Um … see you later?"

"I'm sure. You seem to pop up in interesting places."

Now he clued in to her mood and shot back. "What's that supposed to mean?"

"It means, how long did you know?"

"Know what?" He was confused.

"Know who I am, or that Derek's my brother. How long did you know who I was at the nursing home? And why didn't you tell Derek?"

"I, ah…" Because he didn't want to come across like a stalker, that's why. Before he could put a sentence together, Macy held her hand up.

"Know what? It doesn't matter. All that matters is that I can't trust you." She turned and walked away.

Derek came out and stood beside Thomas, who was still watching Macy and trying desperately to think of a comeback.

"Yeah," Derek said. "She has that effect on people." Together they turned and went back into the house.

They followed Joshua back into the living room, where he started disassembling the camera-television hook-up. "You gotta admit it, Derek," Joshua said. "Things sure are more interesting when she's around."

"Don't go soft on me man. It ain't old times. Besides, it ain't like she's gonna stick around. You bet, once this is done and Vaughn's all squared away, she'll be too good for us again."

"She is too good for us. You know it."

Derek looked down before trying to make light of it. "Amy know you're still hot for her then?"

Thomas sat back in his chair and observed the two lifelong friends as they talked. Slowly, maybe he'd put all the pieces together and figure out what was going on. This bit about Joshua's feelings was a shock though.

"Ah, c'mon man. That's ancient history. Don't be bringing that up again."

"Seriously. What's Amy gonna do when she finds out you and the ex are hanging out Friday night alone?"

Joshua turned to him and got serious. "No one cares about that but you. Don't be stirring things up. That ain't right; don't bring Amy into all of that."

"Fine." Derek stood. "But you started it. See ya later, Tom." He left the room and Thomas turned back to Joshua.

"You and Macy...?"

Joshua rolled his eyes. "Listen, that's really old news. We went together when she was still in high school. Derek's just mad 'cause I told Macy to go. He wanted her to stay. Then she stayed away for good. Until this weekend, I mean."

"Go where?"

"College. University. More school stuff, I dunno. Away from here anyways, away from us. She needed to get outta here, to make something of herself. We was just bringing her down. She denies it, but she's got a big heart, you know? Didn't want to let us down. Especially then."

"What do you mean?"

Joshua finished packing up his equipment and turned to Thomas, taking a moment to size him up and figure out what to say. "There's lots you don't know yet. See, Derek and Macy's old man is in jail. He's been there a while and he ain't getting out for a while. He got hauled off at her graduation. Me and Derek, we just did petty stuff, you know? And the only time we ever got busted was because we didn't listen to Macy. But their old man, he was into some big and rough stuff. Their ma blew everything they had saved for Macy's college on lawyers and stuff, but it didn't work. He went down. Derek and her folks, they all wanted Macy to stick around and help out, 'cause they all leaned on her, but if she didn't get out then, she'd still be stuck here. I broke up with her so she couldn't use me as another excuse. I didn't want to be holding her back. I think Vaughn gave her the money for school, but he ain't never said nothing, though, and she coulda got scholarships and stuff. She was always real smart."

You loved her, Thomas thought. A young man making his girlfriend leave him for her own good; that was pretty impressive. He wondered if he would've done the same. But in his circumstances, people didn't usually have to choose between their family and their futures. One led to the other.

Joshua rose. "I gotta get back to the store." Thomas rose too and together they walked to the front door. Technically, Thomas set his own hours and could basically come and go as he pleased at his job, but he didn't want to stand out that much. The outfit he was wearing already said too much.

"Listen." Joshua stopped at the door. "Don't mention any of this, okay? Amy'd get all bent outta shape, and Derek's still pissed off that Macy only came back 'cause she had to, for Vaughn."

"Not a problem." He paused, then asked, "You think he's happy to see her, though?"

"You bet. But it bums him out that he holds her back. Hearing that she had a hard time getting a job was bad enough, but now this? This a-hole dumped her cuz of her family. Well, Derek takes stuff like that personally."

"Understandably."

"He's gonna be tense for a while. Mostly Derek's just afraid Macy's going to disappear again, but he can't drop the attitude long enough to make peace."

"Huh."

Together they walked down the street and around the corner a few more blocks where they parted and Joshua went back to work. Thomas started walking towards the nearest bus stop, then turned another corner to where his car was parked. Thankfully it was still there, in good condition. He hadn't thought of the implications of taking his own car until it was too late. Usually he came by subway to maintain his cover, but today's call had caught him off-guard. He might as well admit it to himself: He'd only come for the opportunity to see Macy again, now that the nursing-home routine had been disrupted. Not that he had played it well. That was annoying. On the drive back to his office in his BMW SUV, he thought as much about her as he did about the Friday night plan. Maybe a little more.

CHAPTER SEVEN

Macy thought about her lie as she made her way home. Vincent had meant something to her. The pain had faded, but it had left behind an obvious hole she hadn't noticed before him.

Vincent had been the guest instructor for her kickboxing class one night at her gym. She didn't think anything of it until he showed up the next night in the lobby and asked her out. She was standing there in her workout clothes, sweaty, hair messed up and makeup coming off, while an attractive man invited her out to dinner. When they did go out, he seemed so put-together that she was impressed. He talked about his job, his workout routine, his condo, his car, his travels, his everything. It was actually a bit of a relief he didn't want to poke or pry into her life. It was a couple of months before Macy realized she was being pitched to, and by then he had already proposed. She had thought it was a crazy, impulsive thing and said what the hell, never taking it seriously. To be honest, afterwards she realized she just wanted to be asked. It just felt nice to be ... chosen, to be wanted that much by someone so upstanding. So normal.

Who thought she was normal too. Acceptable. Saying yes was the most impulsive thing she had ever done.

Then, one night, he had surprised her at her apartment. He had been planning to introduce her to his family that weekend, and in anticipation of that, he had run a background check on her. By that point, the warning bells had been getting louder in her head anyway, but she still thought it really odd. Even she didn't run background checks on people she dated, and she was a security consultant, for crying out loud. He explained that they couldn't go on, as she had misled him into thinking she came from a good family. She tried to point out that really, he hadn't asked her enough about herself to give him any indication of her family, but he interrupted her and asked for his ring back.

Shame, really. It was a nice big flashy rock. Now she realized it was just an accessory, as she would have been. Or an acquisition, like his job, his condo, his car. Just checkmarks on a list. Still, while she knew she wouldn't have gone through with it, it was nice for a moment to pretend.

Her thoughts of Vincent followed her as she entered her apartment. She stopped a moment, looked around. Usually she enjoyed her space, but today it somehow felt emptier. Macy was fully aware it wasn't the apartment — it was her.

She kicked off her shoes, took a deep breath and tossed her keys onto the counter. She was lying to herself and, as a general rule, she tried not to do that. Too many others would do the job for her. She had felt something for Vincent — maybe not love, certainly not a lasting bond, but something was there, a connection of sorts. At the very least, he had filled a gap she never knew she had. She seemed to be discovering more of those as she got older.

As she took off her jacket, she glanced at her door, remembering one night when Vincent wasn't himself and came knocking. He had been out on the town with some friends, or some people, she wasn't sure which. He didn't seem to have many friends. Regardless, he had had too much to drink and came to her place rather than going home. He was out of sorts, and she had never seen him like that. He was usually so composed. But that night, he had needed her.

He was also drunk as a skunk and she had never seen him like that before, either. Come to think of it, Macy had never seen him lose control of any kind. So it was quite a surprise when he showed up.

He was sweet that night, all lovey, telling her how great she made him feel. How he was going places and he'd take her along. Together they'd conquer, together they'd have a wonderful life and they'd show them all.

Except Macy didn't know who they were showing. Well, she knew who *she* was showing. Everyone who had told her she was just like her family, who had expected her to get pregnant like Amy and flunk out of high school like Derek or drop out like Joshua. True, they had all gotten through somehow, but her good grades and hard work were seen as simply delaying the inevitable. She was Amy's best friend, Derek's sister and Joshua's girlfriend. It wasn't until later that she gave them up, turned away in shame, ran off to university and didn't look back. She started fresh, making it up as she went along, all the while inching towards the life she wanted. One in which she was untouchable, bulletproof.

Vincent seemed to understand, somehow, or maybe she was just so accustomed to playing her part that now she felt more comfortable doing so. She wasn't good at opening up, but they seemed to have similar values, if not backgrounds.

She wouldn't tell him much about hers but, then again, he rarely asked; he wouldn't tell her much about his when she did ask. She assumed this was what a relationship was like with someone like him. With someone not like her.

They both wanted to leave their mark, to see how far they could go. Macy just assumed he was closer to the mark but that night, some of the things he let slip... How he never wanted to be hungry or dirty again. How she made him feel good about himself. How she was good and he was afraid of losing her. She was fairly confident only someone like her would notice or understand without brushing it off as intoxicated ramblings. Which meant that Vincent was like her: a pretender, striving to leave a past behind and reaching for a brighter future, like one in a magazine.

Now Macy walked around her apartment, around the future she had created. It was a nice place, and it was all hers. She had a good job, too, and of course her bike. They were all tangible, which meant they were both real and replaceable. If somehow she lost them, or someone took them away, she could get them again, she knew, because she had managed to get them at least once already. She used that thought to calm the fear that tightened in her belly at the thought of going without again.

Vincent was into things: tangible, materialistic things. He surrounded himself with them. While Macy felt good knowing she could have things if she really wanted to, he seemed to need them. And he wasn't good at needing. After that night when he showed up drunk on her doorstep, he had withdrawn for a while, so she pretended nothing had happened. She recognized his reaction — he didn't like needing her, letting her see him in that condition. It would make her defensive too.

So when he suddenly announced that they couldn't have a life together, standing there in his crisp shirt, pants creased just so, hair with just the right amount of product in it, wearing an expensive brand-name cologne, perfect in his presentation, it knocked the wind out of her. Macy suddenly wanted the messed-up version of Vincent, the one who let his guard down, who had cuddled that night and told her he loved her.

Because in that moment he had made her feel cherished. In another moment he took it away, leaving her with the realization of how empty she felt. How empty she was. Vincent may have only represented an ideal she was always striving towards, but he was more than she'd had in a long time.

Macy reached the window and turned around to view her apartment from a different angle. Now Vincent was using her past against her, against people she loved. Yes, damn it, after all these years, she loved them. Was he punishing her for getting too close, she wondered. She had always thought her family would hurt her if she went back. Now she realized she was the one hurting them. She had brought this to Vaughn's doorstep, literally. She was the connection to Vincent.

And was he really a killer? She thought about Victor, wondered what might have happened if Vaughn had been alone in his room that day, instead of his roommate. Could Vincent hurt Vaughn, or anyone else she cared about, if he didn't get his way? How could she have been so wrong about him?

It doesn't matter, she answered herself. She couldn't give him the chance to hurt anyone else again. There were far more serious things at risk now than just her silly broken heart. Thomas's face came to her mind. No time for that, she thought. She wondered if her big brother would still beat up boys for her. The ache that accompanied the thought made her realize she really did want him to offer. Although Derek approved of Thomas, she could tell. Obviously she couldn't trust herself and her choices anyway. So it was good Thomas had shown her already she couldn't trust him either.

August 6, 1950

Dear Diary,

My adventure has really started! When we got to Ottawa, Vaughn and the others had to make a stop at a tavern. They were picking up liquor for prizes in the bingo. My friend Cassie's parents come over the border here sometimes to go play. They make a big night of it and Cassie stays at my house. There's a bus that goes round the counties nearby and picks up more people. Some folks think bingo is just fancy gambling and gambling is a sin, but I don't mind it. The money goes to orphanages and stuff like that, so how bad can it be if you're helping do good.

Anyway, I'd never been in a bar before, on account of being three years too young still. The boys snuck me inside and we were going to listen to the band after they loaded up the truck, but then the place got raided! They were looking for some people, but I got caught for being underaged. I was put in the paddy wagon and taken to the station. I was some scared and didn't want to call Mama or Papa. I was there all night long, but then, in the morning, a real nice priest I had been talking to in the tavern talked the police into letting me go. Because I'm so young they let me out with just a warning. The priest's name was Father O'Malley. He was real sweet and we had a real nice conversation in the tavern, so it just shows to go you that sometimes talking to strangers is a good way to make new friends, like the boys, who stayed around to wait for me.

Vaughn was there to pick me up. He was real worried about me and he hung onto my suitcase for me. Bobby was bragging about something, trying to make it seem like the police station and the raid didn't bother him none. I think he was showing off some. He's cute too, but more flashy. They still have to make a few pickups so I'm going with them, and we'll see the city. So far they're my first friends here in Canada, plus the priest. Soon we'll go to Montreal and the boys say it's close. But I sure do want to thank Father O'Malley before we go.

CHAPTER EIGHT

"Why are we using these ... walkie talkie things again? Uh, over." Derek's voice blared into Joshua's car, parked across from Vincent's condo townhome.

"Like I told you, it's because cell phones leave footprints," Macy responded.

"What you talking about? They're phones, they got no feet." He was trying to get a rise out of her.

"Are you being dense on purpose? Don't you have better things to do?"

"Don't get snotty with me, I ain't the one talking crazy about cell phone feet."

"I mean, cell phones leave records. Are you high?" Macy switched off and took a deep breath. "Oh look, there he goes."

Joshua raised the small binoculars he had brought but really didn't need and watched a man lock his front door, walk down the steps, get into a silver Audi and drive off. Macy spoke into the walkie talkie again.

"Derek, he's on his way. He should be there in about twenty minutes."

"Roger that."

Rolling her eyes, she checked her watch. They'd have at least forty minutes, which had to be enough time. Looking at Joshua, she gave him a nod, he returned it, and they got out of the car. As they strolled up to the house, Joshua slid off his jacket and held it in one hand. As he reached the unit's top step, he reached for the porch light with the jacket covering his hand and unscrewed it slightly, enough to make it go dark. He reached into his pocket for a lock-picking kit, but Macy got to the door first and used a key. They were inside within moments. Joshua turned his attention to the security system on the wall, but Macy just waved at it.

"He's too lazy, forgets it all the time," she whispered.

They both dug small flashlights out of their pockets and started up the stairs to the main floor. Joshua also put on a pair of thin gloves. His prints were in the system; Macy's weren't. Plus, she had a legitimate reason for her prints showing up at her ex-boyfriend's place. They walked softly and quickly up the stairs, anxious not to disturb the people in the unit below.

The stairs brought them to an open combination living-dining room with a large kitchen that overlooked the space. In a quick glance Joshua noticed it was very neat and tidy. Mounted on the wall was a flat screen high-definition plasma TV that was at least seventy inches wide — bigger than Macy herself. It was framed by bookshelves filled with rows and rows of hardcover books that looked old and untouched. Macy motioned Joshua to the right, and they went down a hallway to the bedrooms. Opening the first door, Macy showed Joshua the home office. The computer also had a flat screen monitor, sitting on a minimalist modern desk. The few files and office supplies on the desk were arranged at ninety-degree angles. There was another television here, a slightly smaller version of the one in the living room. The shelves held trophies and sports paraphernalia of various kinds. Pushing back the black leather chair, Macy jiggled the mouse until the screen lit up.

"He hardly ever shuts it off. Wants everything at his fingertips, and he's compulsive about checking stocks, sports, stuff like that."

Joshua sat in the chair and rolled up to the monitor. "Let's get started. I don't know how long this'll take to download."

Macy pulled the USB key out of her purse she had slung across her torso. "What will this do?"

"This," he said, inserting the key into the drive, "will record what sites he visits, and all the typing he does, which means we get all his messages too. It sends it to a computer I have set up. And," he said as he started typing, slowly because of the gloves, "it's all undetectable. Almost."

"Almost?"

He shrugged. "More and more companies are using stuff like this to watch employees. Especially in banks, high tech, places like that. But this is kinda different, since we'll be at a different location, and our computers aren't linked or networked."

"Cool. Hey, where did you learn this stuff?"

"Night school. Taking some courses, here and there. Gotta do something now that I'm no longer a juvenile de-lin-quent." He drawled out the last word.

"Cool." She tapped him on the arm, and he could feel the smile in her voice. "I'm going to start searching." Macy was at the door when Joshua caught her.

"Hey Macy?"

"Yeah?"

"You have his key."

"Ah, yeah…"

"I'm just saying, you have his key."

"Leave it alone, Joshua." She sounded more tired than threatening or defensive. She was already wrestling with thoughts of her first love compared with her last. She really didn't want to get into details.

He swivelled in the chair to watch her leave as the door shut behind her. The computer screen whirled behind him.

She walked through the apartment silently, trying to re-evaluate the man who lived there, feeling bad about having brought trouble to people she cared about. In her attempts to better herself, she had just made things worse for those at home. Could she have foreseen it somehow in Vincent's choice of decor, his preference for espresso straight up, the way he chose his aftershave by the price and brand, not by the smell? She laughed at herself a little. Obviously she hadn't come as far as she thought.

Twenty minutes later they were done with the computer, and Joshua had joined Macy's search when Derek hissed through the walkie talkie that Vincent had left the scene.

"Damn," Macy said. "Okay, we'll look for just a little longer…"

"No we won't. Derek." Joshua took the walkie talkie out of Macy's hand. "We're heading out. Did you get the tracker on his car?"

"Roger that. Lazy jerk parked in the spot closest to the drop-off. He came to us, he was so easy to find."

Joshua had Macy's hand and was leading her back down the hallway from the main bedroom. "We don't have time to finish, Mace. Gotta go."

"Joshua, we need that stuff!"

"We'll get it another time."

"How?"

"You'll think of something."

They were at the front door and she was still dragging her feet. "Just a couple more minutes!"

He turned abruptly to face her. "You're not getting caught. And right now, you sound like you're about to slip up."

"Fine. Then you think of something." Quickly they retraced their steps, locking the door and screwing the porch light back in.

They were driving away when Joshua spoke again. "You know, back there, you was acting like one of the stupid criminals you used to warn us about."

"Forgive me for not breaking and entering correctly. I'm out of practice."

"I'm saying that you're breaking your own rules."

"Don't I know it."

"Hey, is it really so bad being around us?"

"Joshua, don't."

"No, really, Mace. What's the problem?"

What's the problem? Where to start? How she reached too high, only to be slapped back? How going through her ex-fiancé's home with her ex-boyfriend was a little much? Not to mention Thomas, the mysterious stranger, giving her butterflies — *flutterbies*, Anabelle would say — and complicating things further. "I just want this to be over. I'm worried about Vaughn. Is that so bad?"

She was also worried about her own judgment but didn't feel like mentioning it.

They were silent for a moment. "I don't wanna fight, Mace. I'm just saying … well, what do I know."

A few more moments in silence, then Macy tried to change the subject as they approached the old neighbourhood. "So, you and Amy, eh?"

"Yeah." He stole a glance at her, but she was smiling.

"You love her and Anabelle?"

"Yeah."

The smile was in her voice again. "Good." Joshua pulled over and parked in front of her childhood home. "Joshua." She made him look at her. "Hurt them and I'll kill you."

"Don't I know it." They laughed and hugged as best they could from their seats.

From an upstairs window, Amy watched them until they entered the house. Frowning slightly, she let the curtain fall back. If it were anyone but Macy, she'd be worried. She didn't realize she was playing with the small ring Joshua had given her as she walked down the stairs to find out how the night's activities had gone.

CHAPTER NINE

A week later, Macy was looking forward to what had become her usual Friday night routine. She'd check out the new releases streaming and spend the evening with whichever movie star caught her eye. She was humming as she let herself into her apartment and kicked off her heels. Her big decision tonight would be red or white wine to go with her popcorn. She changed out of her office clothes and put on her bumming-around gear: yoga pants and a t-shirt. *Hmm, maybe a bath before the movie*, she thought as she pulled her hair back into a ponytail, when there was a knock at the door.

She froze for a moment. In the months Macy had been in the apartment, she hadn't had many visitors. The last one had been Vincent, and didn't that turn out well. It wasn't a heavy knock, or an authoritative one, so she knew it wasn't police… Without stopping to think about how she could recognize police knocks, she finally moved towards the door as the second knock sounded.

"Who is it?" she asked as she stood on tiptoe to look through the peephole.

"Thomas." There he was.

She opened the door. "How do you know where I live?"

"Um, hello to you too." He held up a laptop. "Thought you might like to see what the blackmailer has been up to lately." Thomas moved past her into the apartment.

"Well, come on in," Macy said sarcastically, shutting the door behind him, now very glad she had kept her bra on under her casual clothes. "How do you know where I live?"

"Hmm? Oh, Amy told me." Thomas was looking around. Well, he was trying to look anywhere but at her, lest he stare. The pants formed nicely over her behind, and the ponytail was cute, really cute. This casual state was another side of her, besides the open and friendly person in smart dress clothes he had noticed at the nursing home and the tough attitude she projected in her motorcycle jacket and boots.

It was a small, neat apartment, not expensively furnished, but cozy. Muted colours coordinated between the couch, curtains, even the placemats on the small bistro table that stood in the dining room area. He put the laptop on the table before he bent to untie his shoelaces and stepped out of his shoes in the foyer.

"Amy? Why would she give you my address? She gave you my address but not my phone number?"

"Oh, she gave me that too."

Macy was surprised. Amy had been so careful to help shield her and here she was, giving out her home information to this almost-stranger. But if a man asked Amy for a phone number, she'd assume there was romance in the air.

"Then why didn't you call first?"

"Oh, I thought about it. But then I figured you'd say no, don't come over."

"So." Macy stood with her arms crossed in front of him. "You didn't ask because you knew I'd say no?"

He smiled down at her. He liked her this way, dressed down and comfortable. Even in her defensive stance she seemed more relaxed. She must be getting used to him. "Yes."

Annoyingly, that made a certain kind of sense to Macy. It was a smart move. Her brother and friends would have shown up because they wouldn't have thought ahead about calling. Amy was probably leaping happily to conclusions over Thomas wanting Macy's contact information. She knew Amy would be in touch soon for details. She relented and moved out of the way to allow him in.

"So what do we have?" She indicated the laptop.

He was still looking around though. "What, no tour?"

Her lifted eyebrow answered him. "Okay then. Well, I always hate crime fighting on an empty stomach. Have you had dinner yet?"

"No. What information do we have?"

"Always so business-like. Obviously this is your kitchen…" Thomas started giving himself a tour. He noted the packet of microwavable popcorn on the counter. "And this is your living room…" He picked up the remote from the television stand, and scrolled to see what she had lined up. He glanced at the titles, then looked up in surprise at her.

"*The Expendables*, part fourteen? A documentary on Wall Street?"

"Don't you judge me! I had plans tonight, you know!"

"Macy," he said, waving the remote towards the list of shows on the screen, "These were your Friday night plans?" He couldn't keep a straight face.

When he put it like that… "What are you trying to say, Thomas?" She started smiling too. No, wait, she was annoyed at him. She wasn't entirely sure why, but she had to remember to not go soft on him. He had misled her, or at the very least surprised her. That was bad enough, she decided.

"What were you going to have for dinner, by the way?"

Oh. She hadn't thought about that. And it had been a while since her last run to the grocery store. "Popcorn." She was looking at him defiantly now, with an outright smirk.

"Thai. Do you like Thai?" As she nodded, he put the remote back down.

"There's a…"

"I know…"

"I'll just…"

"Number fourteen please. With…"

"A side of sticky rice?"

By this time he was back at the door tying up his shoes.

"How'd you know? Did Amy tell you that too?"

"Because, Macy." he stood up and addressed her very seriously. "A woman of great taste, such as yourself, would naturally have sticky rice. Plain white rice just won't do." He turned and strode out the door.

"Smartass!" she called down the hall after him. He laughed as he walked to the elevator. She chuckled as she shut the door, then was a little annoyed at herself for finding him funny.

Thirty minutes later he was back. She had opened the laptop and started perusing the contents. Together they set the table and distributed the food as Macy filled him in on what she had found so far.

"He's taken some pretty serious hits on the stock market," she said, passing him a spoon for the spring roll sauce. "Thousands, possibly tens of thousands. He checks every day, and he has charts to record every blip. That could be what he wants the money for. He's also speculating in crypto currency, and that's quite volatile."

They sat down and she surveyed the table. "Would you like something to drink? I do have beverages. Water, milk, juice, pop… I don't have beer, which goes well with Thai, but I do have wine."

"Wine sounds good."

"Red or white?"

"Whatever you're having."

She got up again and, after checking the fridge, pulled a bottle of pinot noir off a rack and handed it to him with a corkscrew. "I don't have any white chilled; hope this will do." He opened it as she got wine glasses off a kitchen shelf. Returning to the table, she sat again and continued her report as Thomas poured.

"I can't find any indication of how he found out about Vaughn, or what he might have to tie Vaughn to what happened. But I didn't dig deep. I'll take another look tomorrow."

They were both thinking the same thing. The connection between Vincent and Vaughn was her. Macy chewed her lower lip for a second, looking down and feeling bad. Thomas saw the dip in her chin and reached over to clink glasses with her, forcing her to look up. She gave a weak smile in return. They started eating. "So," Thomas began. "How did you meet this guy? How well do you know him?" He hoped he sounded nonchalant.

She chewed her food while she thought of what to tell him. He already knew her phone number and where she lived. She really would have to talk to Amy about that.

"I met him at my gym. We dated for a while. He was really serious, really fast. Until he wasn't." She shrugged and Thomas didn't buy it.

"So you work out?"

"Don't sound so surprised." Macy was well aware that, despite her best efforts, she still looked more plush than pumped.

He chuckled. "Not what I meant. Sorry, that came out wrong."

She fought the urge to ask him about himself, helping herself to another sip of wine instead. "I'm wondering if this has something to do with his work somehow. He's a financial advisor. I'll look into it more."

"Tomorrow?" She nodded. "Any other plans this weekend?"

"Um, maybe some grocery shopping, so I have more than popcorn in the house. Maybe hanging out with Anabelle for a bit. The gym, laundry, errands, that sort of thing. But don't worry, this is my priority. I'll get it done by tomorrow. You'll get your money back soon. Oh, speaking of, how much do I owe you for the food?" She was afraid she was rambling a little, talking too fast and sipping too much. He was sitting rather close to her.

Thomas's mouth was too full to answer, so he just shook his head and waved her off. When he could, he said, "Don't worry about it."

"Are you sure? Well, okay. Thank you." Damn it, he was being nice again. And he smelled good.

"I would like to get back into his house, though. I know he's going to a charity event next weekend." She knew because she was supposed to go with him. Plans changed.

"The Galaxy Gala?"

"How did you know?"

"I have tickets." Actually, his family was a major sponsor of the event, which raised money for the city's school breakfast program. He usually stayed in the background, rarely even attending such things, but he'd make an exception this time. If she'd give him a chance. Vaguely, he registered the thought that yes, he did want a chance with her.

This was unusual. He was accustomed to being known, to having women want to be with him based on his name, his background, his money. He was used to being afforded a certain amount of respect. With Macy, he got to just be himself, on his own level. The anonymity he had with her gave him freedom, but it also worked against him. Or rather, it made him work. He rather liked the idea of earning her affection and her respect. He tried to sneak another glance at her plush bottom in those yoga pants.

"Well, it may be a good chance to get back into his house again. He'll be out for hours."

"Is that something Joshua and Derek can do?"

"Probably. Why?"

He topped up her glass. "We could go. To the gala. You and me, I mean." He went back to focusing on his food, hoping he had struck the right note of nonchalance.

She dropped her fork. "What?"

He could see he had startled her. Slight change of tactic, then. "You know, see his reaction when he sees you. Mix things up a little. Go on the offensive."

"That's not a bad idea," Macy said. And it would give her an excuse to wear the dress she had bought for the evening, the one hanging in the closet with its tags still on. She hadn't been able to bring herself to return it yet. She smiled. "Bring the fight to him, so to speak. Keep him on his toes." In her head she was already scheduling a hair appointment.

"I'm glad you agree," he said, topping up her glass again. "I'll pick you up at seven?"

"Okay. Unless you'd prefer to meet there? I mean you don't have to go out of your way..." She didn't want him thinking it was a date. This was a business arrangement. For reasons unknown, he was helping Vaughn, and they were working together for that reason alone, she reminded herself.

"Don't be silly. We'll go in style, make a bit of a splash. That way he'll definitely know you're there." She deserved to be treated better than being told she wasn't good enough for a blackmailing jerk. "He'll know you're not alone."

She paused. "Okay."

They looked at each other then, and smiled. The moment held.

When they looked away and shifted, he covered by saying, "Besides, you need something better to do than watch *The Expendables*, part fourteen."

"Hey!" They were teasing now. "What's wrong with my taste in movies?"

"Part eight was the best one. They went downhill after that."

"No way." For the most part, they were done eating. "You have not seen all the movies."

Thomas pushed back a little from the table. "Have too."

She quizzed him to make sure, then they debated the films' merits as he helped Macy tidy up. When the table was cleared and dishes put away, she expected him to turn to the laptop for more business at hand, or leave. Instead, he picked up his wine glass and continued his little tour of her apartment.

Macy was enjoying herself. She was sure the wine they had already consumed had something to do with it, but it had been a while since she'd had company. She found herself relaxing. The nagging voice in her head reminding her to be on guard became fainter with every sip of pinot.

After peeking into her bedroom — he couldn't resist — and bathroom, Thomas returned to the living room and started browsing her bookshelves. She picked up her glass and sat on the couch.

"Wait a minute," she said. He turned to her and sat down beside her. "How is it that you have nothing better to do on a Friday than bring me the laptop? And food? Don't you have someplace to be?"

"Not really." He looked at her again. "Next time I'll call ahead." That would give him an excuse to make more plans with her, but tonight was a good start. Then there was the gala — that was a great development. "I am sorry about not giving you notice I was dropping by."

"No, you're not."

"No, I'm not." They laughed.

Again with the moments, she thought. *Enough of the looky-looks, mister.* But then she found herself saying, "So … would you like to watch part fourteen? I mean, since you're here and all. And you fed me. And my Friday night plans are ruined anyway…"

He laughed and accepted. She made popcorn and he opened another bottle of wine.

Three hours later, after the movie and a discussion of its finer points, Thomas was leaving. She walked him to the door. They were both a little unsteady, after all the wine. He reassured her that he wasn't driving, but taking the subway.

She held the door open, then leaned against it, looking up at him as he stepped across the threshold and stood in the hallway. "Thanks again for the laptop, and for dinner."

He looked down at her. "It was my pleasure. Thank you, I had fun tonight." The low-key evening was the most enjoyable one he'd had in a while. She was good company. "I'll see you for the gala." He turned to walk to the elevator.

She smiled and automatically replied, "It's a date. No, wait, I don't mean it's a *date* date, I didn't mean to say that, I meant, just, you know, I'd see you then…" Macy was babbling and she knew it.

Thomas stopped and allowed himself a smile before turning back. In two quick strides he was back to Macy at the door, where she was still speaking.

"I mean, I know this is just business and all, it's just an expression…"

Without breaking stride he planted one hand to steady the door behind her, and with the other reached out to her face and tilted it up. All her senses went on high alert and she finally shut up. This was bad, the delicious kind of bad. Her breath caught and she found herself leaning forward, just slightly, preparing for his lips to land on hers…

Instead he changed his angle a little and rubbed the tip of his nose against hers before pulling away and blinking.

"Sure," he said when he pulled away. "Just business."

He looked as stunned as she felt as he turned and walked down the hall. She didn't say anything, just watched until he rounded the corner towards the elevators. Once he was out of sight, she stepped back into her apartment, shut and locked the door behind her, then leaned on it.

What the—? A nose rub?

Glancing over the empty bottles of wine on her kitchen counter towards the clock on the microwave, Macy concluded it was too late to call Amy for some insight into what had just happened. She'd call in the morning and they'd analyze it together. Maybe she'd ask Amy to help her get ready for the gala, or at least consult on shoes…

On the other hand, if she talked to Amy about it, she knew what she could expect. Amy would make wild assumptions and start encouraging her to rush in. Maybe she should call Ellie instead. She would advise her to have a fling, then walk away. Maybe she should talk to both of them and divide their advice in half.

Hmm. It had been a long time since she had needed girl talk for something positive. Macy sauntered off to bed without realizing she had never had such thoughts about a business colleague before.

***

A nose rub? What the—?

Thomas shook his head at himself as he entered the subway station and made his way down to the platform to wait for a train. What was he thinking?

He was going to kiss her. He had fully intended to kiss her. He'd really, really wanted to kiss her. But at the last second he'd panicked like a schoolboy. It would've been too easy just to swoop in and sweep her off her feet. So why didn't he?

Because, for the first time in a long time, he had really enjoyed his evening. He wanted more evenings with her. And he didn't want to mess it up, not when it seemed she was starting to relax around him. It would be bad enough once she realized he was keeping secrets from her, that he was helping her family not just because he was Derek's friend but because his own grandfather had given him a mission to protect his family, and the family name, from the blackmailer. He was starting to wonder if there were a way he could keep her from finding out... No, that wouldn't work. He wouldn't be able to keep it up for long once she met his family.

His train came and he entered, standing in the aisle and holding onto a pole.

Couldn't he have grown a conscience *after* he kissed her?

Groaning, he closed his eyes and knocked his head against the pole.

CHAPTER TEN

On Sunday afternoon Macy hesitated at the front door to her childhood home, then rapped and entered without waiting for anyone to answer. The door was always left unlocked during the day, a leftover from the times when both she and Derek would have friends pop by often. Well, more Derek than her, as she spent most of her time following him around, and obviously he still preferred the door that way.

The absence of a scent registered with her as she stepped inside. Growing up, both her parents had been heavy smokers, and Derek had taken up the habit early. Now the only whiff she caught was the lingering ghost of Vaughn's pipe.

Derek was sitting in the living room, flipping channels between sports games.

"You quit smoking?" she asked from the doorway.

He looked up, startled. "Ah, yeah. When Amy and Anabelle moved in. Joshua quit too."

She nodded. "Where is everybody?"

"Vaughn's out for his walk. Joshua and Amy took Anabelle out somewheres. They'll be back soon. They know you're coming."

She nodded again, looking around the living room. Derek was sprawled on the couch. She rocked back and forth on her feet a moment or two before realizing she still had her boots on. It wouldn't have mattered when she was younger, but the place seemed cleaner now. She bent over and took them off, then set them down in the hallway by the front door. She straightened and took a few strides into the room, deciding on the overstuffed armchair. She sat down and took a deep breath.

The last time she had a long conversation with her brother it was held at the top of their lungs, with tears and accusations, and led to a very long silence between them. Macy had finally had it with their dad, said he had gone too far, while Derek, always loyal and big-hearted, tried to convince her to give their dad a break. She just didn't have it in her that time, not seeing her mother so sad again, not with all their money gone to lawyers and bail over the years. Not with her one shining moment they should have cherished as a family poisoned by her father's arrest at her graduation. She didn't think it was fair that he had put them all through it, over and over again, and she'd burst on their behalf.

Macy wondered if Derek was remembering that night too. The next day, she had gotten on a Greyhound bus for university. She took a deep breath, trying to relax. They watched an inning of the ball game in silence. Bit by bit she worked her way back into the chair until finally she was comfortable enough. "You want anything? Just help yourself," Derek said during the commercial, jerking his head towards the kitchen.

"No, thanks."

It was her turn to speak. "So, ah, how's work?"

"Can't complain." They were both looking at the television.

"You? What do you do?"

"Research, mostly. Security checks on employees when companies hire them. Stuff like that."

It was almost a conversation, albeit a slow, well-spaced out one.

"Where you living at these days?"

She told him, hoping he wouldn't bring up how long she had been in town without coming by. He didn't.

They were momentarily distracted by activity in the game, then Derek picked up the thread. "Thomas says he's taking you out next weekend."

Macy was surprised. "Vincent — the blackmailer — he's going to this event thing in a few days and we're going to shake him up."

"It's alright. Thomas is a good guy."

"It's not like that," Macy protested.

"Whatever. Just saying, he's a good guy."

"Whatever." She shifted in the chair. "So, ah, is he coming today?"

"Maybe. Maybe not." He smiled slightly. He actually did know but he couldn't resist a chance to torture his kid sister. She rolled her eyes at his familiar expression.

More activity in the game had them both leaning towards the television. She hadn't watched the Jays play in years, but she did have a habit of turning on hockey games in winter, just for the familiarity. The memories of baseball games, though, were too bittersweet. The good times she had shared with her brother were best packed away like his trophies.

"You ever play anymore?"

"Sometimes. Joshua and me belong to a house league over at the community centre. We play in the park on Ethel Street."

"You should teach Anabelle. Take her out sometime to help you practice."

"Like I did with you? I nearly got you killed! Then Mom nearly killed me!" It had been a long time since they had shared this story, but they both knew their parts.

"It was your first home run, of course I went after it."

"You shoulda caught it then, with your hands not your face!"

"I tripped!"

"You went after every ball like a lunatic."

"Hey I still got — I still have that one, you know."

"Seriously?"

"Yeah. It's put away somewhere." She knew exactly where it was, in the storage bin at the back of her closet, along with her mother's things that she couldn't bring herself to go through.

The back door opened then, as Vaughn came home from his stroll. The others arrived shortly after. Joshua and Amy put groceries away as Macy played with Anabelle. Thomas arrived and joined them just as Macy was getting up to help Amy prepare the fixings for the barbeque. She wanted the chance to chat more than she felt any domestic duty.

Vaughn sat on the back porch as Anabelle played in the yard and the guys prepped the barbeque, which involved standing around it with beers in hand. Once or twice, Macy stole a glance outside. Thomas was standing between Derek and Joshua; they were all of a similar height, Derek the furthest away from six feet tall (*you might say height did not run in their family*, she thought wryly) and Joshua the closest.

While they all wore jeans, Thomas's didn't have work stains or obvious wear. Derek and Joshua were in sneakers, Thomas in leather shoes. The t-shirts the others wore had tiny holes from using them to cushion their hands while opening beer bottles. Macy couldn't tell from where she stood, but she'd bet Thomas's shirt was newer, in better shape. She'd also bet it smelled nice, like he did… She didn't realize she had stopped chopping.

"So I hear you're going out with Thomas on Saturday?" Amy prompted.

"Oh yeah! I tried calling you yesterday."

"Sorry, I had to work in the morning, then Anabelle had a birthday party, then her swim class…"

"No problem. I was just wondering, um…"

Amy started smiling. "Go on…"

"Hey, why'd you tell him where I live? And why did you give him my number? And why didn't you tell me?" Macy playfully aimed her paring knife in Amy's general direction.

Amy was washing and handing tomatoes to Macy. "Oh, don't be so uptight. You need to get out more."

"Next time you decide to play matchmaker, ask me first."

"It worked, didn't it? You got a date."

"Not exactly. Vincent will be at the fundraiser and Thomas already has tickets, so we're going to see how Vincent reacts when he sees me. That'll give Joshua and Derek some time in his apartment too. I'll update everyone after dinner."

Amy was pulling condiments out of the fridge. "Have you seen him since he dumped you?"

"Ah, no."

"He's such a creep. Don't know what you saw in him."

"Are you kidding? On the surface he's great. He's perfect, on paper. And I just…" Macy shook her head.

"You should go out with Thomas." Amy had moved on to plates and cutlery.

"Don't get too excited. It's just business, then he'll go back to his life and…"

"Whatchya mean?"

Macy paused. Amy was always spinning happily-ever-after endings for her, until the actual endings, at which time she conveniently remembered why she never liked the guy in the first place. "Enough from me. Tell me how the wedding plans are going."

They enjoyed their girl talk for a little while longer, during which Macy snuck several glances outside and Amy teased her every time she caught her, then dinner was ready. Everyone found a place in the backyard, either on the steps or in lawn chairs. It was a beautiful day, and spending it having a barbeque in the backyard seemed the natural thing to do. Amy was obvious when she rushed to take the seat beside Joshua, leaving the one beside Macy open for Thomas. He sat and asked a few questions that got the old stories flowing again, especially from Vaughn about Macy and Derek as children. The common theme was Derek always getting into trouble and Macy following him around. But conversation stopped when he asked how their parents responded to their antics. Macy stood abruptly and started gathering plates. Thomas set down his beer and followed her into the house with his plate.

"Hey, I'm sorry if I said something…"

She tried hard not to notice that he came after her when he saw she was upset. She waved him off. "Don't worry about it. It's just, we're having a nice time and I don't want to start anything, you know?"

"Yeah."

Macy shuffled plates around more forcefully than necessary in the thirty seconds it took for her to respond to his look. "Stop looking at me like that."

"Like what?"

"Like, like, like you do. Look, Dad's in jail, Mom's dead, I haven't been around much since."

She thought she'd shocked him and was shocked herself when he just leaned casually against the sink and looked steadily at her. "I know."

"You know what?"

"I know all that."

"Oh." She paused, then turned on the water to fill the sink. "Well, I just don't like talking about it."

"My mom's dead too." He announced this as he reached over and picked up the dish towel. Thomas had shocked her again.

"Oh. When?"

"I was in high school. Dad remarried pretty fast. His secretary, actually. She stepped in to help out with us kids, and well…"

The others started bringing everything else in from outside. Macy and Thomas were quiet until they were alone again in the kitchen, with Amy taking Anabelle upstairs and Joshua, Derek and Vaughn gathering in the living room.

"So, you wanna get matching t-shirts or something?" Macy asked him as she handed him a dish to dry.

"T-shirts?"

She nodded. "Dead Parents Society. Since we're in the same club and all. I mean, I feel we've really bonded now, don't you?"

Thomas chuckled at her morbid humour. "Now who's the smartass?" He flicked the towel at her, and she responded by batting some soap bubbles at him.

They passed the time in companionable chatter, performing the ordinary household chore. Macy tried to wrap her head around Thomas's casual acceptance of her background. He was pretty much seeing her at her worst with the blackmail situation. And he still looked at her in that ... way of his. He moved around and beside her, asking when necessary where this utensil went or that dish should go. He seemed comfortable, far more relaxed than she was. He wasn't running away yet. Oh wait, that probably meant he wasn't interested. Silly her, to think anything of the sort. That would explain the not-kiss. Mentally she chided herself. He was bankroll; this was business.

Thomas was sure he was going to drop something. He was hyperaware of Macy, the space she took up, how her hair fell and how her jeans hugged her bottom. She was so close as he reached around her for the dishes. The more he found out about her, the more he liked her. Hell, by this point he respected her. It made her even more appealing, but brought him into unfamiliar territory. He wanted her to like him back, to think well of him too. Dropping dishes and breaking glasses would not help his cause. He took a deep breath and was distracted again by the scent of her shampoo. She was close enough for him to lean over and nuzzle her neck...

She turned around suddenly, surprising him. "Last one," she said, handing him a cup. He took it with a smile that he hoped masked his thoughts.

Once everything was put away, they joined the others in the living room. When Amy slid back into the room and perched next to Joshua, Macy started explaining what she had found on Vincent's computer. *Back to business*, she thought, and tried not to note anything about how close Thomas stayed.

"Vincent is in debt," Macy announced. "He's living well beyond his means, and can't pay for his lifestyle. Obviously somehow he found out about what happened with the bingo priest and saw it as an opportunity to make some quick cash. Only I still can't figure out what he has, which means it's probably at his condo. Which means we have to get back in. When Thomas and I are confronting him at the fundraiser, Joshua, you go back to his place with Derek and continue the search."

"What do you mean, confront?" Vaughn was concerned.

"Nothing major," Macy replied. "Just gauge his reaction when he sees me again. See if he mentions anything."

"I'll be right there," Thomas said, to reassure Vaughn. He didn't like the thought of using Macy that way, though.

Macy smiled at Thomas thinking his presence would protect her. "There will be no physical confrontations. I met him at my gym. He instructs the martial arts instructors. This will be a chit-chat only. Really, it's just to buy you some more time at his place," she nodded at Joshua and Derek.

They discussed the plan for a little while longer, then Macy and Thomas got ready to leave. He walked her down the block to her bike, trying to look casual. She just assumed his car was nearby. He bunched his hands up into fists in his pockets; he was trying not to think about kissing her goodbye and hoping she didn't think he was an idiot for the nose rub.

Macy was thinking of that nose rub and was glad she hadn't spilled everything to Amy after all; she would have been unbearable and even more obvious. They chatted about the plan, then about the gala, then about how they really should be going, then they chatted a little more. Eventually they parted, Macy driving away on her bike, Thomas turning to walk further down the block until she was out of sight before he turned and walked in the opposite direction, to where his car was really parked.

September 18, 1950

Dear Diary,

I haven't written in a long time because something terrible has happened. It all happened so fast, then we were trying to get away, and now — well. As Mama would say, start from the beginning.

That day, my first full day in the city, the boys were still picking up stuff from different clubs around town. The last one was close to the police station, just around the corner, and I was thinking, wouldn't it be nice to see the friendly priest again, to say a proper thank you. The boys drove over to the police station so I could go in to ask where I could find him, and they parked in the back, off an alley that we found. Vaughn and I were walking over to the police station while Bobby and John stayed in the truck. Down the lane we saw a taxi pull up, and out of the back of the police station who came out but Father O'Malley himself. He was walking over to the taxi and I was afraid we were going to miss him, so I called out. He stopped and looked at us, then he smiled and started walking towards us.

Suddenly — wham! A couple of men stepped out of the alley and shot him! I screamed. One of the men pushed the priest into the cab, got in and took off, but the other one heard me and started running at me. Vaughn had already started running back to the truck, shouting for Bobby to start it up. But I couldn't move. I just screamed.

The man was about to get me when Vaughn grabbed me and pulled me into the truck, then Bobby — Bobby hit the gas and ran the man over. John was in the back. He said later the man never got back up. Bobby must've killed him.

We drove out of the city straightaway. I thought we should go to the police, but Bobby said he had just killed a man, he couldn't go. John wanted to get home to Montreal right away, but the other boys wanted to hide out or lay low, as they said, back on Vaughn's parents' farm. We drove to Montreal and dropped John off, then drove back to Vaughn's place in the country. We drove most of the night.

Vaughn's folks were very kind, putting me up so we could figure out what to do. We didn't tell them what happened, of course. That I had gotten us into a sticky situation and then Bobby killed a man — to save me.

The boys kept their ears open for local gossip and started hearing some things. A while later John showed up, saying we was wanted by the police for kidnapping the priest, 'cause no one saw him again, and the criminals — the mobsters — wanted us for what happened to the man Bobby ran over. John stayed at Vaughn's parents' too, until we all decided it would be safer in Toronto. The boys say it's Canada's biggest city and it'll be easier to hide there, since they never went that far on their bingo pickup routes but they were known in Montreal and over the border as far as my hometown, Malone.

So we all came to Toronto. The boys are in a boarding house two blocks away, and I'm in one for girls only. They got jobs, and I'm a waitress at the Golden Wing diner a few blocks away. They're still my only friends here, but some of the girls at work are nice, especially Vera. I can't tell them what happened, of course. I can't tell anyone, ever.

When I save up some I'm going to send some home to help Mama and Papa. But the money is different here, so I guess I'll go to the bank and ask them to help me.

Well, I guess I made it to the big city. Still feel real bad about what happened to the priest. He was a nice man. I bet his family misses him.

I have to go — Bobby is waiting to walk me to work. He's been doing that, says he feels protective of me now. Vaughn doesn't talk to me much. He got real quiet after what happened. I bet he's disappointed or mad that I just stood there and screamed. If I had stayed quiet, or if I had run too, Bobby wouldn't have had to kill anybody, and we wouldn't have to hide here.

I miss my family.

CHAPTER ELEVEN

A corsage? Should he have brought a corsage instead? Thomas wasn't accustomed to second-guessing himself and decided he didn't like it. He brought his hand up and knocked on her door.

She opened it a moment later, and her face lit up when she saw the bouquet in his hands. His face lit up when he saw her. He said hello and handed her the flowers, stepping into her apartment. Macy turned from him to walk into the kitchen and gave him a glance at the back of her gown, which he liked just as much as the front.

"Gerbera daisies! Red Gerbera daisies! How wonderful! I've often thought red roses were overdone." She was rummaging for a vase, smiling. "Come in! Thanks!" Macy was nervous and trying not to look at him. Trying not to stare at him, actually. He cleaned up real good in a tux. She fixated on the flowers.

She was obviously unaware of the sight she was, doing something as domestic and routine as filling a vase with water and arranging flowers, while wearing an ice-blue evening gown that complemented her strawberry blonde hair perfectly. It was piled in an artful mess of curls to frame her face but leave her neck exposed. The dress had halter straps that left her shoulders bare, and it tucked in at her waist before flaring out to fan to the floor. With the flowers taken care of on her dining-room table, she strode over to him. He blinked a few times as she approached before it registered she was obviously in high heels.

"Thank you!" She hugged him quickly, catching him off-guard.

"Ah, you're ah, you're welcome." His arms moved a little too late to hug her back before she floated away from him. He caught one of her hands and gave her a twirl. "You're stunning." She laughed. "And those are some serious heels."

She hiked up the skirt of her gown a couple of inches to show off the four-inch silver stilettos. "All the better for kicking blackmailer butt, m'dear." She was still grinning.

"Not terribly practical," he said with a smile.

She looked at him with a steady gaze. "I have four-inch metal weapons on my feet. I feel prepared."

He laughed. "Indeed. Shall we?" He bent his arm and gave her his elbow. Macy picked up her evening bag and they sauntered out into the hallway.

She had to focus on her key to lock the door. Macy hadn't expected the flowers but they delighted her. She also hadn't expected him to look so… Handsome, yes. Dashing, no. Yet there he was in a tuxedo that fitted him perfectly, and suited him too. His blond hair was slicked back, making it darker and exposing more of his face than his usual waves did. He looked grown up and serious and when he offered her his arm the jacket tightened across his shoulders, showing how wide they were, and she had to suppress a giggle when she felt his bicep under his sleeve.

His family car was waiting at the curb outside her apartment, with a large man in a dark suit standing in front of it. Thomas muttered quickly, "Macy, this is Woodley Edelstone. Woodley, this is Macy." Woodley, his driver, tipped his hat and opened the car's passenger door. "Er — what?" Macy was already being ushered into the back seat but waved at Woodley and called, "Um, hello!"

"Pleasure to meet you, miss," Woodley said as he shut the door after Thomas. Macy noted a British accent, then turned to look at Thomas, now sitting next to her.

"Oh, relax. Woodley's an old family friend. He's just doing me a little favour tonight. Aren't you, Woodley?"

From the front seat Woodley replied, "Yes, certainly, sir," before closing the partition between him and the back seat. Macy turned to stare at Thomas again.

"Gee, I'm glad it's not a limo. That would have been a little much." She rolled her eyes before sitting back.

It was a 1936 black and silver Bentley. Woodley liked British cars. He was a little eccentric, Thomas said, and shrugged. "This way he gets to drive one of his favourite cars and we don't have to Uber."

"Well, I guess it could be worse," Macy said. "It could be the Batmobile."

"Is it just me, or does it feel like we're going to the prom?"

"Sorry, I skipped mine." She'd skipped hers because her father was taken away in handcuffs in front of her entire graduating class as she was giving the valedictorian speech. She'd had more things on her mind than spiking the punch bowl, and the other kids weren't talking about the usual dramas — they were all talking about her. She had sat at home with her mom, while Joshua and Derek drank in the backyard and Amy got pregnant with Anabelle in the backseat of her loser boyfriend's car.

"Then I really should've gotten you a corsage."

She laughed at the remark, and the sound made him smile.

Macy was beginning to get a little tense as they neared the gala, trying not to chew her lower lip and mess up her lipstick, but really wanting to. She hadn't seen Vincent in months, and didn't know what to expect — not just from him, but how she would react. The car was slowing down now.

"So, any ideas on what to say to him?" She was businesslike again, or trying to be.

"We'll play it by ear. Don't worry." He squeezed her hand. "It'll be fine." He kept his hand on hers and she didn't seem to mind. The warning voice in her head had obviously decided Vincent was the bigger problem tonight.

Woodley pulled up to the front entrance then came around to open the door. Thomas stepped out first, then offered her his hand. Getting in and out of cars in a gown and heels was never easy, and Macy appreciated the help. She tried to manage as gracefully as possible. Just before they entered the large converted train station, they stopped and looked at each other. They smiled, straightened, and joined the hundreds of others already inside.

After entering the foyer, they were greeted by the event organizers and ushered inside. With Thomas guiding her, they bypassed the lineups with ticket-holders on either side of the room, walking directly into the main lobby instead.

It was a warm night and neither had brought a jacket, so they ignored the coat check and proceeded to the first room, an antechamber. The lights made designs dance on the ceiling as a local band played. Rather than push their way to the bar, Thomas sidelined a waiter and politely requested champagne. They listened to the music until their drinks arrived, then moved on.

The next room had different music, different food and different people. The largest room, with the dance floor, featured a DJ and a bar in the centre.

Some time later, they had made a full circuit and finished their first flutes of champagne when they arrived back at the entrance. Every time they passed a banner with his family name on it, Thomas tried to distract her or smoothly turned them the other way. She registered that many people knew him but seemed surprised to see him there. He politely introduced her to everyone and they chatted as they moved from food station to food station, sampling hors d'oeuvres as they went. Eventually they made their way back to the main ballroom. He gave their empty glasses to a passing waiter and they were deciding their next destination when she noticed Vincent at the bar.

Thomas felt her stiffen. Macy tapped him on the arm and tilted her head. "He's there, at the bar."

Thomas turned her so her back was to the bar and he could take a look over her shoulder. In the process he had to slip an arm around her waist and hold her close, whispering into her ear. "Hmm, the one next to the woman in red?"

Macy had to sneak a peek; she pretended to flip her hair back and whisper into Thomas's ear, leaning close. "Yes, that's him."

He looked down at her. "Ready?" She nodded.

Thomas took her hand and together they approached the bar. As she came closer to Vincent, Macy felt … actually, she felt very little. Once they were in front of each other, Vincent looked over.

"Macy! What are you doing here?"

She looked at him and thought, *Oh baby, I'm so over you. Huh.*

"Hello, Vincent."

She stared at him for a moment, a slight smile on her face, a slight raise in her brow. *He's trying too hard*, she thought suddenly. *He has to work at being cool*, she concluded. From the hair with too much product and the muscles that had been preened over in a gym to his booming voice that made him the centre of attention, she thought he was rather lacking. She could see why she'd found him attractive, originally, but was glad she didn't anymore.

Not too subtly, Vincent checked her out from head to toe. "Ahem," Thomas interrupted, as the arm he had around Macy involuntarily flexed. "I'm Thomas." He extended a hand to Vincent. As they shook, Vincent's date, the woman in red, spoke up.

"Hey, I know you. I recognize you from somewhere…"

Thomas turned to her and cut her off. "And you are?"

The tall, skinny woman smiled widely and extended her hand. "Melissa Combes." Macy tried hard not to roll her eyes as Melissa, with her streaked, unmoving hair, leaned towards Thomas in her tight, low-cut dress and held his hand longer than the shake required. Vincent didn't seem to notice.

"So how do you two know each other?" he asked Macy, who gave him a dazzling smile of her own.

"Well, after the last conversation we had, I took your advice and started looking into my family background some more. Thomas here is helping me."

"Oh, I know what you mean," Melissa said loudly. Her manicured hand flitted back towards Thomas. "Aren't you sweet, helping like that. Genealogy is so important!"

"Yes. If you're breeding livestock." Macy deadpanned, staring at the woman.

Thomas had reclaimed his hand and now placed it in the small of Macy's back. "I'm just helping Macy with a little ancient history. It's always nice to have friends." He said the last part with a direct look at Vincent, before turning away and looking at Macy again to share a smile with her. "Well then, must be off. Nice to meet you." Together they turned and walked away.

They made it a few paces before Thomas commented, "Livestock?"

"I could have said dogs. Or horses."

"Too true."

They claimed another set of champagne flutes from a waiter, then subtly checked over their shoulders to see what Vincent was doing. After watching them walk away, Vincent turned back to the bar. After a few more minutes, Macy stepped into the lobby to call Joshua and Derek and notify them that contact had been made. Thomas tried to stand in the doorway to keep an eye on Vincent while not losing Macy in the crowd.

While Macy was on the phone, Thomas's sister-in-law Theresa spotted him as she walked past. They were chatting, and Thomas's brother Will came over with his and his wife's coats when Macy got off the phone. Thomas made the introductions, then added, "But they were just on their way out."

"Oh, that's too bad," Macy said.

Will was helping his wife with her coat. "Babysitter curfew! But it was nice to meet you."

"Nice to meet you too."

Theresa gave Thomas a kiss on the cheek before turning to Macy. "I don't know how you did it, but I'm impressed you got him here. Goodnight!" She gave a smile and a wave as she and her husband left.

Thomas drained his glass as Macy laughed at him. "They seem nice." It was also nice to be introduced to people in his life, although she tried not to notice. Theresa looked as polished as Melissa had looked processed, but the sparkle in her eye was real. As they turned back towards the ball, she asked about his family. He explained his siblings, then his nephews and nieces, chatting until the music grew too loud for easy conversation. Back inside, they tried to keep Vincent in sight. It was relatively easy to do, since he spent most of the night at the bar, but eventually they gave up on surveillance and just enjoyed the night. Macy tried hard to remember it wasn't a real date, while Thomas tried hard to make it feel like one.

In a few hours, when her feet were sore and his jacket and tie were off, they found Woodley outside and rode back to her building. Thomas again gave her his hand to help her out of the car, and walked her to her door.

Macy fiddled with her evening bag. "You know, it's amazing how hard it is to find something inside such a little bag."

"Little?" he teased. "I could run away from home with what you have in there."

She laughed. "Got 'em!" They were quiet as she put the key in the door and turned it. She opened it slightly, then turned to look at him. He had gone quiet and was looking at her too. His hand came up and caught one of her curls that had slipped and now trailed down. He brushed it out of her face. She moistened her lips, about to either thank him for the evening or invite him in, she wasn't sure, when the door opened suddenly from the inside and a strong arm grabbed her, pulling her in.

Vincent flung her, propelling her further into the apartment. She stumbled and almost fell, grabbing a chair at the last second to steady herself. His back turned to the door and he tried to slam it shut, but he hadn't noticed Thomas on the other side. Thomas pushed it back open and grabbed Vincent's arm.

"Don't."

Vincent blinked, reassessing the situation. "Oh, so it's like that now, is it. The little gold digger got you too."

"Don't speak to her like that."

"Vincent, what the hell are you doing here? How'd you get in?"

"With this." He sneered and showed her a key.

"What the — I never gave you a key!"

"I have ways, you know. Just stay out of my way and nobody gets hurt."

"Are you threatening me?"

Vincent sneered again. "We'll see."

"No, Macy, he's not." Thomas looked Vincent full in the face. "He's not threatening you. Because nothing is going to happen to you. Or your family. He's not going to do anything." Thomas was a few inches shorter than Vincent, and as he looked up slightly at the taller man he kept his voice deep and low, calm and steady.

Vincent shot him a look full of disdain. "We'll see," he repeated. He spun on his heel and left.

Thomas shut the door behind him with a big push, then locked it loudly. There was silence for a moment, before Macy exclaimed, "Derek and Joshua!" She retrieved her bag from where it had fallen on the floor and dug out her cell phone. With a few beeps she had Derek on the line and was telling him Vincent was on his way back.

"Okay," Derek said. "We think we got something anyway. Tell ya tomorrow." They signed off.

Thomas had taken a seat at her dining room table. "Why didn't you tell them what just happened?"

Macy shrugged. "Derek might have done something stupid, like wait around for him."

"And that's stupid, how? He's just protecting you."

"And I'm protecting him. Derek's got too many priors for an assault charge."

Thomas nodded.

"He has a key that I never gave him," Macy said suddenly. "I'll change the locks tomorrow. The bastard made himself a key!" Anger was replacing her alarm now that her adrenaline was subsiding. She kicked off her heels and paced a few steps, her dress pooling around her feet, obscuring them.

"I'm sleeping on your couch tonight, then."

"I'm sure he won't come back tonight, I'll be fine…"

"Macy." Thomas was taking off his shoes now. "I'm sleeping on your couch tonight."

"Thomas, you've done more than enough, really, that's too much."

The jacket with the tie stuffed in a pocket was now slung over one of her chairs, and the cufflinks clinked onto the table. "Macy, I'm sleeping on your couch tonight."

"Okay, this is really getting out of hand. You bankroll us, you, everything you did tonight, then when he was here you stepped in…"

"Macy." He was now in the corridor between the bathroom and her bedroom, searching for a linen closet. He opened the door when he found it and pulled out a sheet.

Seeing what he was doing, she sighed. "Is there any way I can talk you out of it?"

"Yes. You can spend the night at your brother's, or you can come home with me. To my guest room, I mean."

She took a big, deep breath. "I'll get you a pillow."

He was spreading out the sheet on the couch when she returned with a pillow and a blanket. "I need to say it again; you really don't need to go to this much trouble." Thomas took the pillow and blanket from her and placed them on the couch before turning to her and holding her arms in his hands.

"Macy, I'm…"

"…sleeping on your couch tonight," they said together, then both smiled.

She stood up on her toes to give him a small kiss on the cheek. "Thank you. For everything."

He rubbed his thumbs along her arms in a small movement. "You're welcome." He bent down and rubbed his nose against hers, as he had after their movie night. That made her giggle, which made him smile.

A little while later, after he had called Woodley to tell him to go home, Thomas was settling in on the couch when Macy called out from her room. "Thomas?"

"Yes?"

"I really liked the flowers."

"I'm glad."

"Goodnight."

"Goodnight."

Macy tossed and turned for a little while, thinking. She had never seen Vincent act like that before. Drunk, just that once, but this was so out of character, almost out of control. It struck her as … the word that came to her was desperate. Even grabbing her was very strange for him. Not only did he know he could seriously hurt her, given their size difference and his martial arts abilities, he always seemed too contained to stoop that low. She wondered what would have happened if Thomas hadn't been there. She didn't want to think about it. Thomas seemed pretty steady, not backing down or running away when things got tough, and things seemed to be tough all around her. She wondered if she had started trusting him after all.

She also wondered what had really happened to Victor, and suddenly she could see Vincent killing someone while in that desperate state. Her stomach recoiled at the thought. This wasn't just a trip down memory lane anymore; this was real, life and death. Then she thought about both Vincent and Thomas, wondering what she felt or didn't feel for each in turn. Wondering how she had been so completely wrong about the first, and how could she trust she wouldn't make the same mistake with the second. Maybe the problem wasn't Thomas himself, but her. Maybe she was thinking too much. Most likely. In fact, very probably. Finally deciding this was a matter for some girl talk and she would call Amy and text Ellie in the morning, she rolled over and fell asleep.

CHAPTER TWELVE

This was getting serious. It was time to tell her. Thomas shifted a little on the couch. Now she had been introduced to his brother and sister-in-law, and she obviously knew the family had some connections, thanks in part to the blackmailer's date. How could the guy have passed up Macy for that? Macy, who was … so many things. Tough on the outside, tough but not hard, but inside so fun and full of life. Caring and responsible, definitely; smart and ambitious. Beautiful, too, inside and out, as far as he could tell. And he wanted to find out more. He wanted to be the one to make her smile, and laugh, and shield her from anything that brought her down. He didn't have words for what he was feeling, he just knew he wanted to be there.

Thomas heard stirrings from Macy's room. Her bedroom door opened and she emerged, already showered and dressed, her hair still wet. He sat up and she stopped in front of the couch.

"Good morning," she said. "Pancakes?"

"Sure! Good morning."

He had taken off his tux jacket, vest and shirt to sleep in his undershirt and pants. As he stretched, his arms flexed and revealed biceps and shoulder muscles Macy didn't know the name of. She steeled herself to look away from his well-developed upper body and turned towards the kitchen, thinking of the well-developed lower body she had already noticed when he wore jeans at the barbeque. *He definitely doesn't skip leg day.* As she turned, there was a knock at the door. She took a quick look through the peephole then opened it. Macy and Thomas stared as Joshua walked through.

"Morning Macy, Thomas."

"Ah, good morning, Joshua. Um, what's up?" Macy started shutting the door, still staring at Joshua as he entered the apartment. Thomas started getting dressed in a hurry.

"We found some stuff at Vincent's house last night. Derek wanted you to see it right away. Oh, I also brought the laptop. Derek's got it. He's right…"

Derek didn't bother knocking but walked right in, making Macy jump back in surprise. "Hi, Mace. Hi, Thomas." He paused and looked around. "Nice place."

Thomas froze in mid-position, his shirt behind him, his arms partially in. Macy stopped and stared at Derek too. Then they looked at each other, each registering the lack of shock his presence caused the newcomers. Thomas shrugged his shirt on and started doing up the buttons as he took a seat at the dining room table.

"Okay, I guess pancakes for everyone," Macy muttered and started a batch as Joshua and Derek sat at the table and made small talk with Thomas about the apartment and the gala.

When breakfast was ready, Thomas got up to help Macy set the table. Once they were all seated, Macy started right in.

"So what did you find?"

Both Joshua and Derek had full mouths, so it took a moment before Derek answered her, talking around a bite of pancake. "Photocopies. Someone wrote about the priest's murder and he has copies."

Joshua reached into the laptop case and pulled out a few sheets of paper to pass to Macy. She placed them between herself and Thomas so both could take a look. They quickly scanned them. "It looks like…" Macy started.

"Journal entries of some kind?" Thomas suggested.

"It looks like…" she said again, thinking hard.

Joshua and Derek looked at each other and shrugged. If Thomas didn't have the right answer, neither would they.

"Damn it! What is it?" Macy said again, starting to tap the page. Suddenly she snapped her fingers and, without a word, got up from the table and rushed to her bedroom. The three men looked at each other before putting down their forks and following.

They found Macy crouched on the floor, her head hidden from view as she rummaged in her closet. "It looks like…" Her voice was muffled. She started hauling a large bin out of the closet.

"…something from…" She had wiggled the bin out now. She threw off the lid and started pulling out various things, searching for something specific that was apparently at the very bottom. The baseball that had been Derek's first home run nearly hit him in the face as she tossed it over her shoulder; he caught it in a hurry. Joshua was socked in the stomach by Macy's favourite childhood stuffed bunny. Thomas, in front of the bin by now, was unceremoniously handed a stack of papers without her even looking up. Macy was so deep in the large bin that when she came up suddenly with something in her hands she landed with a thud on her butt.

"Grandma's diary!" she exclaimed in triumph.

In her hands was a large shoebox. She opened it quickly and pulled out a small, old book. The men gathered around her to peer over her shoulder.

"It was in Mom's things, but I didn't really go through it. Let's see... What are the dates on those pages?"

Joshua dashed back to the dining room and returned with them. "The first one is August 4, 1950."

Quickly Macy flipped pages until she found the one. Joshua silently handed her the photocopies. She paused for a moment, comparing the two.

"Yup. They match. The bastard got this from me. It's been here the whole time. Listen to this." She started reading aloud from the small book in her hand.

August 4, 1950

Dear Diary,

Today's the big day, I'm finally 18! Mama and Papa both say I can leave home now. If I have to get a job, I'm going to the big city! Well, not the big big city — Mama and Papa say New York City is just too big, they'll only let me go if I stay in nice places, so I'm gonna try Canada. It's close and must be real nice. Maybe Toronto or Montreal. Montreal might be neat, cause it's French and all. It'll be like going to Paris but I can still come home to see everybody. I've been looking forward to this for so long and now it's finally here! I'm sooo excited! I'm packing my suitcase and leaving first thing tomorrow morning. Look out big world!

Macy shifted on the floor as she turned the page. "And here's another."

August 5, 1950

Dear Diary,

Well, I did it. This morning I left and started hitching. At first it was people from home who picked me up and took me a little ways, but then a different car pulled up. A really nice guy hopped out and asked if I'd like a lift. His name is Vaughn and he's from Canada and he's really cute! He's going to Ottawa but says he can take me to Montreal after. He's with his cousin Bobby and a friend named John. They're all really nice. John is riding in the back so I can sit up front with Vaughn and Bobby. We stopped for lunch and Vaughn bought me a cheese sandwich and a lemonade. He said I should save as much of my money as I can for the city. We'll be there soon, and Vaughn says he'll take me out to see the sights. I don't even miss home yet, not one bit.

Macy paused and looked up at the group. Derek was the first to respond to the slump in her shoulders. "He went through your stuff? What a jackass." He sat on the floor beside Macy and pulled the diary to him, bumping her a little with his shoulder in a friendly way. His cheer-up gesture touched Macy, who smiled.

"That's not the only thing he did," Thomas said, then filled Derek and Joshua in on how Vincent had surprised them the night before, courtesy of a key he had made himself that Macy didn't know about. Thomas was aware his tone was angry and didn't care. He disliked Vincent more and more.

Joshua was sitting on the bed. "Mace, you got a key to his place, but you didn't give him one for here?"

Macy shrugged. "He was rude to a waiter."

"What?"

"The night I was going to give him a key, he was rude to a waiter, and I couldn't do it. Besides, he liked his place more than mine, so we spent most of our time over there."

"Well, now that we have the evidence, he's got nothing. Case closed," Joshua concluded.

Macy looked up from her seat on the floor. "Not quite. Are these all the photocopies you found? Because there's more in the diary, so if he copied the whole thing, then he still has something. And we have to get Thomas's money back from the first drop."

"Oh yeah, right, sorry."

"So how do we do that?" Derek asked.

They thought a moment, then Macy snapped again and was up in a flash. She scurried back to the dining room, grabbing the laptop and turning it on. "We need something on him," she said.

The men retook their seats around the table and resumed eating their cooling pancakes as she searched. This time, when she discovered what she was looking for, she smiled and leaned back. "Got it."

Forks paused as they looked at her expectantly.

"Part of his debt problem, besides living large, is a few bad deals he made for clients. I think he used some client money to buy some risky investments and now has to cover the loss without anyone at work finding out, or he'll probably lose his job, if not get charged. We just need to isolate that data somehow, or find some information, some connection, to prove it, then we blackmail him into giving the money back." Her smile grew wider and was joined by others around the table.

"To Macy." Thomas toasted her with his coffee. "Mastermind criminal."

They laughed and finished their breakfast, all in a relaxed good mood.

CHAPTER THIRTEEN

Once Joshua and Derek left, Thomas excused himself to freshen up in Macy's bathroom. She laid out a facecloth and a new toothbrush from her last dentist visit, then took her phone into the living room to arrange for a new lock on her door. When she got off the phone, Thomas had taken the plates to the kitchen and was loading up the dishwasher.

"This is getting to be a habit," she joked as she joined him in tidying up.

"Are you saying we have to stop meeting this way?"

She laughed and flicked the dish towel in his direction. He grabbed it with one hand and, after a moment's pause, pulled her to him. When she was close, he dipped his hand into the sink's soap bubbles and flicked some at her, getting her hair a little wet. They joked for a little while longer until everything was put away.

"What are you doing today?" Thomas asked as he pulled on his shoes, preparing to leave.

"I have to wait for the locksmith, so I guess I'll just hang out here for a while. You?" Macy leaned against the kitchen counter at the edge of the foyer. Thomas straightened.

"I may have a way to follow up on that hunch of yours, about Vincent using his work accounts for his personal use."

"Oh?"

Thomas smiled. "Let me check it out first, then I'll tell you. I don't want to get you in trouble or get your hopes up."

Her eyebrow raised. "Get me in trouble? Exactly what are you doing that could get me in trouble?"

He just smiled again. "Call you later?"

"Alright." Now the eyebrow was down, but she didn't look happy. "Be careful."

That stilled him. "You worried about me, Miss Macy?"

She straightened, hands on hips. "It's not you. It's me. It's my nature." The eyebrow was twitching again.

A smile spread across Thomas's face. He leaned over and kissed her. No preamble: He just leaned over and kissed her.

It was a light, slow kiss, the kind initiated by someone who could enjoy kissing as the main course, not a rushed appetizer. Only their lips touched at first; then, as the kiss deepened, their hands sought out each other, and their bodies leaned together. His fingertips found her waist, her hands, his shoulders.

When at last they pulled away, it wasn't very far. Both felt heady. Macy, on tiptoes again, brushed her nose against his, making Thomas laugh suddenly, then he pulled her close into a hug and held her for a moment. "Talk to you later?" he muttered into her hair. "Talk to you later," she replied to his shoulder.

Eventually he turned and left, leaning back to give her another quick peck on his way out. Well, it started as a quick peck. Macy smiled as she eventually shut the door behind him. Oh yes, it was definitely time for some girl talk. By the time she moved from the foyer into her living room the smile was a full-on, shit-eating grin. Only the mess in her bedroom, with her childhood mementos splayed over the floor, tamped it down a little. She stood, leaning against the frame for a while, looking at the items. The baseball. The bunny. The diary. The rest of the contents she hadn't pulled out. Maybe it was time.

She mulled the thought over. It didn't cause the usual reaction; didn't feel like a punch to the gut; didn't make her clench her teeth. She waited a moment more. No tears came to her eyes, no pain in her chest. Yes, it was time.

But first… She picked up her phone and called Amy. "Hey, it's Mace — are you busy tonight?"

"No, why?"

"How's this sound — drinking, dancing…"

"And bad decisions? I'm in!"

They laughed over their shared mantra, then determined where and when to meet up. Macy would go over and get ready with Amy, just like old times. As she hung up, she reflected that she felt like a teenager again. Ah yes, all those years ago, they didn't seem very far away after all. She walked back into the bedroom, stood in the doorway for a moment, then took a big, deep breath.

Then she sat on the floor to sort through her past as she waited for the building superintendent to arrive with a new lock for her door.

June 30, 1951

Dear Diary,

Well, it's happened, just like Vera said it would. Bobby proposed. He has it in his head to go over the border and sign up to go fight in Korea. Says Canada is too boring now, and besides, we have to fight the Commies. Vaughn's going with him, to keep him safe I figure. With them signed up we don't have much time. Bobby says he wants to marry me before he goes because who knows what will happen. I don't know why they're going at all! We're going to city hall tomorrow, before he has to leave next week for basic training with the army. He and Vaughn signed up, but not John, although you can tell he wants to. They've been talking about it since the war started last year.

I'm going to ask Vera if she'll come with me, and John's girlfriend Barbara will be there. It'll be nice. I wish we had time for Mama and Papa to come too, but with the boys needing to report to the army, we have to do it quick. They may die over there, and then wouldn't I regret not getting married when I had the chance? We may have to get special permission from a judge at city hall, since I'm still not twenty-one, but the war and my parents being in the States should be good enough reasons.

Oh please, Lord, please forgive me for what happened with the priest, and please bring the boys back home safely.

It'll be hard, them both gone at once. They aren't the only Canadians going, either. Men from all over the country are going to help the U.S.A. Vera says we should try to get better jobs while they're away. John has a beer and liquor delivery company now, isn't that rich? We can see if we can get in there, maybe in the office, or at the plant where Vaughn and Bobby work.

I'm doing the right thing, I'm sure. It will be nice, I'm sure. I wish Mama were here to talk to.

CHAPTER FOURTEEN

Thomas wondered how long it would take before his family heard about this. He was sure everyone had heard about his gala date with Macy, thanks to his sister-in-law. His brothers, sister, father and grandfather had, on occasion, made use of their various connections in different ways, but Thomas usually tried to avoid it. In this situation, though, he recognized he could do things Macy and the other guys couldn't. They didn't have access to their very own security team.

Still, asking the team to look into Vincent's work records wasn't exactly kosher. The request was so unusual he finally had to admit it was for a girl; once he said so, his family's head of security, Walter, was all too glad to help. Walter had watched him grow up and, like many other long-time employees or associates of the family business, had a fondness for him. Thomas felt about sixteen years old while explaining his request to someone who felt like an uncle. Still, in the end, he got the information he needed. Macy was right: Vincent was tampering with his work accounts. She had good instincts, a good eye, he thought, as he approached his front door.

It was known as a garden home. It looked like a brownstone, in a fashionable district downtown, a couple of blocks off the main thoroughfare and away from some of the noise and lights. He lived in the main floor and basement, and a young couple had the unit above his. Well, technically, the upstairs unit was his as well, as he owned both, but he had a management company handle the landlord duties so he could retain his autonomy and friendly relationship with people who didn't realize they were his tenants. Most of the block was his, actually. He had roomed with a friend in one of the units during university, and never really felt like leaving, so as they became available he bought them, one by one. He liked to think of it as his collection.

The neighbourhood had gotten quieter over the years since he graduated; over time, most of the students moved out, and when the church on the corner became an official biker place of worship, a strange sense of order seemed to settle over the area. The coffee shop knew his preference, as did most of the restaurants, and many of the shopkeepers would wave as he went by. It was on one of the main subway hubs, so transportation was never a problem, and the record shop was one of his favourite places for a Saturday afternoon, while the library was for Sundays.

It was a little like Macy's neighbourhood, actually. He pulled out his key and opened his front door. He wondered how she had spent her day. He had kept his phone off while on his errand; he would have to turn it on again and give her a call. He stepped into his foyer and shut the door behind him.

He still had one hand on the door when he heard the contained roar of a small bike's engine. Thomas kept it there and cocked his head for a moment, listening to be sure. He opened the door when he heard the hurried footsteps. Macy pulled up short, her hand about to knock, surprised at the sudden movement. It didn't keep her still, though; she barrelled right in and shut the door behind her.

"Do you have an alibi?"

"What?"

"Where were you tonight? Why isn't your phone on? Do you have an explanation for where you were?"

"Hi, Macy, nice to see you. Come on in. Oh, how do you know where I live? Amy again? That little meddler…"

She pushed beyond him and past the door that separated the foyer from the rest of the house. "The police are on their way. Can you explain where you've been for the past few hours?"

Macy stopped a few steps down his hallway, whirled around and looked at him. Several thoughts raced across Thomas's mind — invasion of privacy, illegal snooping into a corporation's private computer systems and using his family resources to do so being the most prominent. No, apparently he didn't have an alibi.

Seeing the look on his face pushed Macy into action. She kicked off her shoes and commanded, "Take off your shoes." Then she started to strip him.

"Wha — ah, Macy, this is a little fast, don't you think?"

She pulled his shirt out of his pants and started to unbutton it. "I should be out drinking and dancing and making bad decisions, buddy. Instead I'm here. The least you can do is get naked."

"Huh? I mean, not that I'm complaining, but really — will you respect me in the morning?"

She had his shirt off now and he had kicked off his shoes. He slid off his watch and handed it to her. Macy tugged at his belt and he yelped. She looked at him. "I won't respect you if I have to bail you out of jail. Now, close your eyes, do your duty and think of your country." With one pull she had his belt off. The next second the doorbell rang.

They both froze. Macy whispered, "You've been here with me all evening." His watch, shirt and belt in one hand, she messed up his hair with the other and disappeared further into his house. Thomas stared after her, then called out, "Coming!" as the doorbell rang again.

He waited another moment then returned to his front door and opened it. Yes, there were two officers on his stoop.

"Hello, can I help you?"

"Mr. Labson?"

"Yes?"

The older of the two, shorter and rounder, said, "Thomas Labson, of the Labson family?"

"Yes." Thomas pulled the door behind him mostly shut, hoping Macy couldn't hear the conversation from behind the bedroom door.

"Sorry to bother you, but we've had a complaint. Seems someone claims you committed vandalism on his property."

"What?" Thomas's shock was real.

"Can you tell us where you were tonight, sir?"

"Ah, um, I was here."

"Can anybody verify that, sir?"

"Ah..." At that moment the door behind him opened and Macy peeked out.

"What is it, honey? Oh!"

She opened the door and stepped forward. Thomas's shock deepened. Macy was wearing his shirt, and little else. It fell to mid-thigh on her, and her legs were bare. She had only done up a couple of buttons, and she had messed up her own hair too. She padded forward in bare feet to stand by his side.

"Is everything okay?" She looked worried.

"Sorry to trouble you, ma'am. Do you know Vincent Brannen?"

"What did he do now?" She looked from the cop to Thomas in wide-eyed suspense. He tried to reassure her.

"Nothing, darling, don't worry. Just, just go back to bed. I'll handle this."

She had come up and wrapped one arm behind his back. His went around her shoulders instantly. They fit. It was nice. Reluctantly he let her go and watched her walk away, her tousled hair sashaying along the way. The shirt draped over her curves and hinted at them nicely. Sighing internally, he turned back to the police.

He had to clear his throat to get their attention. Apparently they liked his shirt too.

"It seems we have a bit of a delicate situation, gentlemen. You see, my girlfriend…" Thomas gestured over his shoulder in the direction Macy went, "was Mr. Brannen's fiancée, and he seems to still have … shall we say, issues?"

They nodded and he continued. "We ran into him at a function last night and he didn't react well to seeing us together. He threatened to do something, but I really didn't take him seriously. Apparently, I was mistaken."

They were nodding some more. "That's fine, sir. If we need you to come down to the station to make a statement, we'll let you know."

"Thank you, officers. Sorry to bother you with something so trivial. Good night."

Thomas watched as they got into their cruiser and drove away. He shut the door but looked through the window for a few moments to make sure they didn't come back. Macy's bike engine would still be warm, betraying their story if they checked it. Finally, he took a deep breath and stepped away.

He pivoted and started walking through his house, looking for Macy. He made it a few steps into his hallway before coming across her shirt on the floor. A few steps more, and outside his bedroom door, lay her jeans. This was getting interesting.

Oh, who was he kidding. He was interested the moment he spotted her in the hallway of the nursing home. She had been there, in the back of his mind, for quite some time. Now she was here, in his home. Wearing little clothing. In his bedroom.

Thomas hesitated a moment before opening the bedroom door. His nightstand lamp was on. Its soft glow illuminated the room in warm shadows. Was that — yes, yes it was, beside his belt on the floor. He looked over and found Macy on the bed. The lamp was behind her and she was definitely not wearing a bra. She had done a good job of denting the pillows and putting the sheets in disarray. His breath caught as she straightened up.

Macy moved from a lounging position to a kneeling one. She sat back on her heels and looked at him in anticipation.

"Are they gone?" she asked in a quiet voice.

"Yes," he responded in kind. A few heartbeats passed. She looked at him standing in front of her shirtless, staring at her. His wavy dark blond hair flopped over his forehead, thanks to her frantic efforts in the hallway a few minutes earlier. His blue eyes glinted in the dim light. His ab muscles pulsated with his breath, and his hip bones hinted at what was under his jeans. He looked at her like he had never seen her before. He looked at her like she was delicious.

She ran her tongue over her lips to wet them. She was suddenly aware, acutely so, of being half-naked in his bed. He had been in trouble and she had come running. Without thinking. And she knew she'd do it again.

"How'd you know?" he asked, his hands on his hips, his legs wide.

"Derek called. He couldn't get in touch with you, your phone was off... He and Joshua were still watching Vincent, knew he was up to something..."

"So you came."

Macy nodded, not trusting her voice. Another moment and she tried. "I should go."

Now it was Thomas's moment to be caught.

"Stay," he said simply.

She blinked a few times. He took a few steps closer. Then her finger was crooked, beckoning him nearer, and he closed the gap between them in a hurry. Her tongue moistened her lips again, this time for a different purpose.

As he approached the edge of his bed, she leaned forward. Her tongue flicked forward, licking the treasure trail just below his navel, the thin line of hair that led below his belt line. Macy heard his gasp. She kept her hands on her thighs but moved upwards with her mouth.

Her tongue traced a trail from his navel to the middle of his chest, then she broke to the left, circling his left nipple and nibbling just a little with her teeth, before doing the same to the right. She lost count of the number of times his breath caught. Macy's heart was racing and she was busy shutting off her brain. Her mouth continued upwards, to his neck, before Thomas's hand caught itself in her hair and pulled her head to the side. He looked at her with heavy lids, swollen pupils, then his mouth came down on hers.

The kiss would have been crushing if either had any breath left to give. Thomas's empty hand slid the shirt off her shoulder, traced her outline before pressing her to him, bringing her ever closer. He needed her; he needed her now. Her body agreed.

He grasped her elbows and raised her above him, so she was standing on the bed. He pulled back to survey her above him. She was glorious. He nuzzled her neck, then pulled her close with one arm behind her as the other slid to the front to undo the buttons of his damn shirt. He managed one, two, maybe three before impatiently pulling it down to puddle at her feet. She stood there, above him, in just her gray panties with pink polka dots that he wouldn't register until the morning, when he handed them back to her.

Now it was his turn. His tongue traced a line from her neck down to her right nipple, where it caught and held. He faintly registered her breath changing before he moved to the left. Then both hands were around her waist as his head moved down.

Macy moved back on the bed to draw him forward to join her. They both knelt in front of each other, caught up and lost in one another. Thomas's hands swirled over her abdomen, her hands caught on his shoulders. His pants button was popped, then Macy slowly slid them down over his slim hips. Thomas stood again to let his pants slip to the floor before kneeling again before her. Macy ran her hands over the outline of his butt in the tight boxer briefs before running them up the inside of his thighs. His hands found hers and held; he kissed her again and held her for a while. Then Thomas was defining her outline with his hands.

His fingers toyed with the band of her panties. He traced their outline before dipping in, first at the top, then at the sides. Each movement took her breath away. She tried to remember where her hands were and reciprocated with movements of her own, over his body. At one point he pulled away, whispering hoarsely, "Macy." He held her away from himself for a moment, until she responded, "Thomas." Then it was alright, then it was understood.

Her panties slipped off the same time as his underwear, then their fingers found each other even as their tongues kept exploring each other's mouths. Thomas laid her back on his bed, and as one hand caressed her, the other positioned her and spread her hair against his pillow so she'd be comfortable. Macy's hands clasped onto his back and drew him near. Just as he was about to, she drew back and looked at him with questioning eyes. His right hand fumbled with the nightstand drawer until he opened it. Thomas rummaged through by feel, paying more attention to kissing her, trying to get his brain to engage. Finally he pulled out a condom. She guided his hands after they ripped open the foil packet. Together they placed it, then they were ready.

Thomas's hands took hers above her head on the pillow. He looked at Macy as he entered, as her breath caught, as she arched slightly to draw him closer. Their blue eyes met and held. Macy's hands curled around his and her body moved to match his.

He moved slowly, enjoying every millimetre, every second. Thomas forgot how to breathe. They both did. Then they were moving, faster and faster until... Even then, even after, they held on. Thomas stayed in place as Macy traced her hands up and down his back. Their hearts had to return to earth. Once they did, they looked at each other. Macy lifted her head off the pillow slightly, just enough to reach Thomas's nose with hers, and gave him a little rub that made them both smile. Thomas knocked his nose against hers before burying himself in the crook of her neck.

Eventually he slumped to the side, and she moved. "Bathroom?" she asked, and he pointed in the general direction. She scooped up his shirt again and slipped it on as she treaded softly to the bathroom. Thomas rolled onto his back, slid the condom off and slipped it into the trash can by his nightstand. In a couple of minutes Macy came back and crawled back into bed beside him.

"Hi," she whispered.

He whispered back, "Hi."

She nuzzled into the crook between his shoulder and his neck, her arms going around him as his went around hers. In a few moments, without a word, Thomas's hand reached out and shut off the light.

"Goodnight, Macy."

"Goodnight, Thomas."

They held onto each other through the night and into the next day.

CHAPTER FIFTEEN

Thomas woke up when Macy padded back into the bedroom after a trip to the bathroom. He smiled and stretched as he reached for her. "Good morning."

"Good morning," Macy replied. Thomas rolled over her, making her giggle, and went to the bathroom to brush his teeth. She had obviously found the spare toothbrush he had set out; sometimes he wondered if dentists knew their part in romances.

He rejoined her in his bed. He liked that, seeing her in his bed. He tried not to read too much into it, but elementary, on a gut level, he knew. His phone on the nightstand started chirping — his alarm for the workday morning.

"Hungry? Would you like to go out for breakfast before work?" he asked between placing kisses along her neck while his hand stretched down her side.

"That ... sounds ... great," she replied, losing her breath when he started nibbling her ear. Macy pushed him back onto the bed and started her own nibbling. They took their time, exploring each other in the daylight, enjoying and savouring without as much urgency as the night before.

Some time later, they dressed and headed out. After locking the door, Thomas pocketed his keys, then took Macy's hand as they walked down the street. They chatted about the neighbourhood on the short stroll to the nearest diner. He held the door open for her and they were waved to a booth by a waitress who recognized Thomas. After asking for coffee, they scanned the menus, then ordered when the waitress brought their cups.

Macy folded the menu closed and set it aside. Sitting up, she put her elbows on the table, laced her fingers together and rested her chin on her hands. "So what were you doing last night before I turned up?"

Thomas pushed his menu away too and leaned back. "You were right. Vincent is dipping into his accounts at work and has some losses to cover. He's covered it up but it won't be hard for someone he works with to figure it out."

"And how did you find this out?" Macy kept her tone even.

Thomas smiled slightly. "I have my ways."

That earned him a cocked eyebrow. He changed the subject, knowing Macy was letting him off the hook. For now.

"So … how did you get into your line of work?"

She chuckled softly. "When we were kids, Derek and Joshua were always getting into trouble. I kept seeing ways they could do things without getting caught. The few times they actually listened, things worked out. With my dad's history, I already had a bit of a background in certain legal issues, shall we say, by the time I went off to school. It's sort of a puzzle, finding the loopholes and plugging them before someone else does."

"A puzzle?"

She nodded and took a sip of coffee. "Actually, that's what I'd like to do one day: be a security consultant with my own shop. Show companies how to improve their security by breaking into them, exposing their weaknesses and helping them fix them, things like that."

"That sounds interesting. Really interesting, actually." Thomas leaned forward and sipped his coffee.

They chatted more about her plans once the food arrived and they tucked in. Thomas also learned that Vaughn had helped her financially with school, and in return she helped him out now.

"I finished reading my grandmother's diary too. Seems Vaughn has a little explaining to do," Macy said smiling. "It was shocking, really. Wait till Derek reads everything."

From the discussion about her family, Macy swung the conversation over to his, finding out more about his siblings, parents and grandparents. "So, is your grandfather about Vaughn's age, would you say?"

Thomas tried not to look alarmed at the connection. "I guess so."

"And you work with your family, is that right? What is it, exactly, you do?"

Thomas shovelled a forkful of omelette into his mouth to give him time to think before answering. "Brewery," he finally muttered. "Nothing interesting."

Macy just nodded, then waited for him to chew and swallow. "You ever going to tell me?" she asked softly.

Thomas looked at her for a moment and was about to reply when the waitress reappeared to sweep away their plates and offer the cheque. Thomas picked it up automatically and took it to the cash register to pay, where Macy joined him.

They held hands on their way back to his place, and before Macy drove off on her bike they kissed goodbye. Thomas watched her go, then pulled his cell phone out.

"Walter? Hi, it's Thomas. Yes, I always forget, you know… Listen, you know the guy I needed information on last night? I need a favour… Are your boys around today?"

***

After work that night, in a different area of town, Joshua and Derek were hunched in Derek's car, down the block from Vincent's place. They were about to drop off the counter-blackmail letter but wanted the go-ahead from Macy first.

She finally answered her phone once she got to her apartment building and parked her bike. Joshua was updating her when they spotted activity in front of Vincent's house.

"Ah, Mace, you're not going to believe this. A big black van just pulled up, and two guys … wow they're huge! They're going up to his door. Yeah, it just opened, he just opened it. The guys just pushed their way in. Well, like football players, or bouncers. Huh? Ah, no, no name on the van. Can't see the plate either… Oh, here they come." He and Derek instinctively ducked down as the van passed their car. "Okay, we're going … talk to you soon."

Joshua and Derek got out of the car and walked quickly up to Vincent's door. Derek reached out and knocked before Joshua could swat his hand away.

"What?" Derek said. "He knows who we are. I wanna meet this guy."

A minute passed and Derek knocked again. Finally they heard a soft voice. "Who is it?"

Joshua and Derek looked at each other before Derek responded. "You know who we are. Open up."

"I already told the other guys, you'll get your money! I'll pay you back!"

Joshua and Derek looked at each other again. "Ah, what other guys? The guys who just left?"

"Yes! I'll give the money back and I won't do anything else to that jerk ... I mean, I'll leave Thomas alone!"

"Did the other guys tell you when to pay it back by?" Joshua tried to sound threatening not curious.

"Yeah, yeah, in three days. Same drop as before, I get it."

"Okay then." Joshua and Derek turned to go, but Derek swung back suddenly and pounded on the door.

"And you'll leave my sister alone too!"

"Macy? That bitch—" Derek pounded on the door again. "I mean, I mean, yeah, of course. I'll leave her alone."

"If you don't, we'll send the other guys back!"

"Okay, alright, whatever you want! Just, just go away, leave me alone."

Joshua and Derek walked back to the car. As Joshua waited for Derek to unlock it, he asked, "Ain't he some kind of karate expert or something?"

Derek nodded, "Yeah, Macy said something like that."

"It weird to you he was so scared like that?" They got into the car.

Derek just shrugged and started the car.

"Who'd you think the other guys were?"

Derek turned to look at Joshua before pulling away from the curb. "Man, I got no idea."

CHAPTER SIXTEEN

Macy entered her building and, as she passed the mailboxes, decided to give it a shot and detoured. Maybe she had gotten mail lately. Ellie had confirmed via email that she was off travelling again, so a postcard was possible. She had flutterbies in her stomach from Thomas, so anything was possible.

As she plugged her key into the slot, her eye caught something — the door to the basement was open. It was set into the wall beside the mailboxes, so she saw it every time she walked through the lobby, but she had never seen it open before, so it attracted her notice. Pulling her key from her mailbox lock, she went over. Tapping the door with her foot, she opened it further.

The light from the mailroom shone down the stairs, illuminating just the first few steps but leaving the bottom in darkness. Macy sensed something wasn't right. Everything in her being screamed at her to leave, to turn away. At this point in a movie she'd be yelling at the character to get out of there. Of course, at this point in a movie the character would be wearing nothing but her underwear and carrying a dead flashlight, and would not heed Macy's warnings at all. Still, she reached out with her right hand to try to find a light switch.

She found it, flicked it on and lost her breath.

The sight of the body sprawled at the bottom of the flight of stairs would have caused many others to scream, but Macy wasn't a screamer by nature. Instead, she crouched down and looked around. Once she determined she was alone, she launched herself down the stairs.

It was Mr. Lee, her superintendent. He lay at the bottom, upside down so his feet were on the stairs and his head was on the floor. His eyes still open, his head and neck at an unnatural angle. He looked surprised, and there was a scuffmark on his shirt. Macy took a quick look at her surroundings, then knelt to check his pulse. Not really knowing what to do, she first pressed her fingers against his wrist, then, not finding anything, put them to his neck. His neck, bent at an odd angle…

Macy straightened, shocked. Then she scrambled for her phone and called 911. After blurting out something about finding someone not moving at the foot of a flight of stairs, then giving the address, she looked up the stairs to the light coming from the mailroom. Then she looked back down at Mr. Lee. She sat on the floor, beside him, not wanting to leave him alone like this. After a moment she leaned closer and looked at the smudge on his shirt. It was definitely dirt, and the length … there was a bit of an outline…

Shocked again, Macy sat back up, then looked up the stairs, back down at the body, and up at the door again. She scrambled to stand up, then scurried up the stairs. Yes, it could have happened that way. Her elbow hit the door and it bounced back after a slight swing. She stepped back, into the hallway by the mailboxes, now staring at the basement entrance.

Someone had kicked Mr. Lee down the stairs. Someone who could land a high kick to his chest with enough force to knock him through the door and down the steps. Someone like a desperate part-time martial arts instructor who was known to come to her apartment when she wasn't there. Someone who had given her cause to ask Mr. Lee to change her lock.

Wait — someone who came to her apartment when she wasn't there… She remembered the day she'd thought of Vincent's cologne, when she found her bedroom door shut.

The police found her there a few minutes later, still staring at the doorway.

February 17, 1952

Dear Diary,

Bobby's back from Korea. He was injured over there, so he spent some time in a hospital in Germany first, but he's home now.

I know I should be grateful, and I am. I'm very grateful he came home alive. But he's changed. I hope it's just the leg wound, but he'll always walk with a limp from now on.

That wouldn't be so bad if he weren't always in a bad mood. He's been home a couple of weeks now, and he hasn't even talked about going back to work. He's drinking more too.

I know so many women whose husbands won't come back from the war, but in a way mine didn't either. The bad side of him is getting worse.

Meanwhile Vaughn still writes to me. I told him that John and Barbara got married too. Only Vaughn is still single, although he could have his pick, and he will again when he gets home.

I should be glad I got my chance to get married, even if we haven't had any babies yet. They will come, God willing.

Unless God hasn't forgiven me for what happened with the priest.

CHAPTER SEVENTEEN

Several hours later that evening, Macy found Amy in the main bedroom of her childhood home, searching through the closet. After finding Mr. Lee and giving her statement to the police, Macy had considered cancelling her plans with Amy again, but she really didn't want to be alone at her apartment. Macy said hello and gave Amy a quick update. They had spoken earlier on the phone, and Macy had told Amy about finding her building superintendent. She still felt a little numb.

She had also told Ellie, in an email, and was starting to regret that. Without the context Ellie would worry, and she was too far away to do anything. Macy felt bad for distressing her friend. She wasn't sure how she was supposed to feel after finding a dead body, and that made her think of Thomas and wonder how he felt when he found Victor. And that made her worry about two dead people in such a short period of time, and she wondered about coincidences.

Macy flopped onto the bed. It gave her a good vantage point from which she could offer her opinions on Amy's clothing choices. It used to be her parents' room. It had been pale pink back then, her mother's favourite colour. Now it was purple, for Amy. Macy remembered watching her mother get dressed up too. Not often, but on the few occasions her mother went somewhere special. She suppressed a frown. It hadn't happened often enough. It was usually when her dad had a court date or was coming home from prison. Her mother glowed around her father; it was the only time she did. Her mother had said he was her soulmate, but then again, she was a hopeless romantic.

Her mother said a lot of things that stopped making sense to Macy once she figured out how much hurt she also carried, along with all the hope. All the faith in the world wasn't going to change her father, who in his own way was also a dreamer, Macy was starting to see. Always looking for the next big break, so he could take care of his family, give them everything he thought they deserved. But he could never see that all they ever wanted was just him.

Macy could deal with having friends' parents not let them play with her; then, later, being the laughing stock of the school, the one pitied and doomed by other people's expectations. She'd always had to earn people's affection and respect. Yes, it had been hard, but it had helped her become who she was. Her conscience spoke up and pointed out that she was anonymous in the life she had created for herself. She told her conscience to stuff it and take the night off. Her mind flickered back to Thomas as she trailed her finger along the blanket. She had to be careful not to make a habit of turning off her brain. Flutterbies were one thing, the future was another.

She continued tracing a pattern on the bedspread, thinking about Mr. Lee and her mom, life and death and how fine the line was in between, how rarely you could capture the moment one moved into the other. She definitely wanted to go out tonight, to be surrounded by noise and energy.

Amy brought her back to the present. "So?" She called from the closet without looking at her.

"So?"

"So." Amy glanced at her. "What brought this on?"

"Why do I ever need drinking, dancing and bad decisions?"

"Men?"

"Yup."

Amy put down the hangers in her hand, on which hung the first two choices. "So?"

"So?"

"You did it, didn't you!" Amy jabbed a hanger in Macy's direction. "You slept with Thomas!" she announced with a grin.

"How — well, yeah, okay, I did, but how did you know?"

"You're kidding, right? 'Bout time. So how was it?" As she spoke, Amy held the first shirt up, saw Macy's scrunched nose, then replaced it with the other shirt, which received a so-so assessment. She turned back to the closet. "Details, girl!" When a moment went by with nothing from Macy, Amy called, "That good, eh?" She turned back with more selections and saw Macy's grin. "What are you wearing? Stand up." Amy gestured again with the hangers.

Macy stood and turned to show Amy what she was wearing: a royal blue shimmering shirt with a slight cowl in front that hung just right with her dark-blue skinny jeans. She had taken the subway over, so she didn't have to wear her motorcycle boots, but the ones she did wear looked similar; they went to her knees and gave the sophisticated top a little more edge.

"So why are you here with me and not somewhere with him?"

"What do you mean? I had plans with you."

"Honey, you haven't been laid in how long? Why did you pry yourself off?"

Macy laughed at Amy's straightforward talk. "What, I'm supposed to spend every living moment with him now that we've had sex? That one's nice."

Amy tossed the selected shirt onto the bed behind Macy, then twirled to show off her form-fitting pants. "This okay?"

"With that top? Sure." Macy got up and went to the small set of speakers, played with the iPod until some music came through, then returned to the bed.

Amy picked up the shirt and put it on, a black off-the-shoulder that sparkled. Rummaging in the closet again, she finished off with strappy black heels.

They moved on to hair and makeup. Amy had a dresser with a mirror in the room so they didn't need to cram into the hallway bathroom as they had before so many high school dances years earlier.

"You're not gonna keep a man that way." Amy waggled a blush brush towards Macy.

"We've had sex once, well, twice, then there was — ah, we spent one night together!" Macy rolled her eyes. "Sex does not a relationship make."

"You're doing it again!"

"What? What am I doing?"

"You're thinking too much. Just—"

"Amy." Macy looked at her in the mirror. "Are you about to tell me I have to stop thinking to keep a man?"

"It's not bad, you know," Amy said as she swirled powder over her face. "It's not a bad thing to want to be happy."

Macy rolled her eyes. "I can be happy without a man, Amy."

"Whatever you say. But look at me, me and Joshua been together a long time now. That's happy. You ain't happy."

"I'm not happy because I don't have a man?" Macy deadpanned.

"You do now! Just don't screw it up." Amy said it matter-of-factly.

Several thoughts came to Macy's mind. Oh yes, this was the voice of reason she'd heard in the back of her mind when Vincent had proposed. She had been surrounded by this type of thinking for most of her life, with both her mother and best friend dreaming of romance and Prince Charmings. She picked up her lipstick, thought again, put it down and walked to the door. From there, she hollered downstairs for drinks. That was the kind of happy ending she was after right now. Joshua obliged, bringing up a beer for each of them. Macy hadn't had anything but wine in ages and got a laugh when she asked him for a lime wedge.

Finally she turned to her friend. "Amy, is your love life the only thing that does make you happy?"

"What are you talking about?" Amy applied black eyeliner to her right eye, then her left.

"Well, what about work, or friends, or stuff you want to do, or whatever. What about the other parts of your life?"

Amy stood and stared at her. "There you go again. Blah blah blah, Miss University." She bent forward to get closer to the mirror as she applied mascara. Her open mouth and her frozen position made her next words harder to understand. "Not everybody can be like you, you know."

Macy took a hard swallow of beer. "What are you talking about? You finished high school…"

"I got my GED after Anabelle."

"But you could always enrol as a mature student, maybe try a college program…"

Amy shook her head and Macy protested, "What? You could! After the wedding, maybe Joshua can help with Anabelle, or maybe you could take a class when she's in school. Are you going to be at the diner your whole life? Don't you want more?"

"More what?"

Now Macy was playing with the makeup containers on the dresser, picking them up, reading names, opening lids to see colours. "More, I don't know. An easier life? You work hard, you're always on your feet, your pay sucks, but if you went to school, you could get a better job. You'd have more opportunity, more choices."

Amy was almost done, but not quite. The hair needed more spray. "Choices? What am I gonna choose? I got my man, I got my kid, I got a place to live. I'm good." She took a swig of beer, then tipped it towards Macy. "You? Would it kill you to have a man around?"

"It hasn't been that long!"

"Long enough!"

"Will you stop trying to marry me off? I'm fine, I don't even know what this thing with Thomas will turn into. I don't know what I want it to turn into."

Amy shook her head. They were both swaying and bopping to the music now as they sipped their beers.

"I mean, I made such a huge mistake with Vincent—" Amy responded to his name with a muttered, "Rat bastard." Macy continued with a smile, "And now with Vaughn and the whole blackmail thing going on, I don't really know what I'm doing."

"What's there to know? Boy meets girl, boy and girl bonk, boy and girl live happily ever after, unless smarty-pants girl blows it or boy becomes another rat bastard."

That made Macy laugh again. "Hey, at least you think I'm smart."

"Don't make me smack ya. I'm not, you know, you always been the smart one. Thomas is smart too. He likes ya."

Macy pushed aside the little glow she felt to address Amy's admission. "You're not stupid yourself, you know!"

Amy dismissed her comment with a wave of her hand. "So?"

"So again?"

"Details, girl!"

Anabelle was at a sleepover, so they turned the music up and hollered for more drinks. Joshua dutifully complied again. As they sipped, they danced around the room, pulling out accessories and trying them on, bracelets and earrings, necklaces and scarves. Traditionally Derek tried to lay low when the girls got gussied up; his kid sister was never appropriately dressed in his eyes. Apparently that was still true, because he stayed firmly planted in his chair in the living room, eyes glued to another game on the television.

Finally the beers were done and they were ready. Joshua waited at the bottom of the stairs and whistled as they came down. Derek heard them coming down and hollered from the living room, "Here comes trouble!"

"Drinking, dancing, bad decisions!" They said together as they left the house. Joshua drove them to a nearby bar and received a very enthusiastic kiss from Amy as thanks before she got out of the car. Macy, already on the sidewalk, hollered, "Get a room!" in good fun. Together they sauntered into the club and proceeded to act like teenagers.

The next morning, when she woke up in Anabelle's room, Macy's pounding head had her thinking she maybe wasn't so smart after all. But she smiled when she glanced at her phone and saw that Thomas had called.

CHAPTER EIGHTEEN

Macy walked back into her apartment building slowly, pausing outside the mailroom. The yellow police tape was still there, across the basement door. She wondered how long it would stay there. She wondered if Mr. Lee's family knew yet, or even what family he had.

That made her think of Victor, at the nursing home. And that led to thinking about her mom, how she had died shortly after her dad went to jail for the last time. Her high school graduation was the last time the whole family was together.

As Macy made her way through the lobby, up the elevator and to her apartment with its new lock, she thought about her parents. It was a true romance, she had to admit. Her father, always looking for one more score, to give his family everything he felt they deserved. Her mother, believing in him until the end, until it was too late.

Macy's heart hardened a level when her father was arrested during her valedictorian speech, but it hardened even further when her mother fell ill and died. Her father was escorted to the funeral by deputies. The cuffs were still on as he knelt beside the coffin Vaughn had paid for. Macy blamed her father for her mom's death. She blamed him, she thought now, as though he had caused the cancer that took her mom, and not the daily two packs of cigarettes her mom had smoked most of her life.

Giving herself a shake, Macy let herself into her apartment using her new key. She had thought Vincent would take her away from her bad memories. Instead, he was creating new ones. If she were smart, she'd keep that in mind with Thomas.

But sometimes she was tired of being smart. Everyone around her listened to their hearts, and they survived. Mind you, they didn't have what she did, but they were happy enough. So what did she want?

She pulled out her phone again. She hit redial to call Thomas back.

"Hi, it's me."

"Hi there."

"How's it going?"

"Good, you?"

Macy hesitated. "Well, something interesting happened."

"Last night with Amy?"

"Um, no, before that." If he was in, he was in. Macy took a deep breath and told him about finding her superintendent dead.

In the pause after she stopped talking, she was sure she had lost him. There was always a line normal people didn't cross. She could, because she didn't belong in polite society. But usually there came a point at which people decided she was too much to handle. Well okay, only some people, she tried to remind herself. Some superficial, immature, judgmental people she shouldn't have trusted in the first place. But it was a hard lesson to learn, that she couldn't share all her details with everyone. So here it was, the point at which he realized she came with a family of criminals, blackmail and murder. The point at which he cut bait…

"I'm on my way." Thomas hung up.

Macy wasn't quite sure what she expected, but she knew that wasn't it.

Half an hour later he was in her apartment striding with purpose into her bedroom. "You're staying with me tonight."

"I'm what?" She wasn't used to taking orders.

Thomas whirled around, held her by her arms. "You've seen two deaths in the past two weeks. You needed a new door lock. There's some blackmailing going on. Forgive me if I'm a little concerned, but you're not staying here."

He stared at her long enough for her to take him seriously, then turned back to her bedroom. "Now, then, do you have an overnight bag?"

Macy stood for a moment, just staring at him and his take-charge attitude. "Um, yeah, ah, it's in the closet…"

Thomas turned to the closet, threw the doors opened, and dove in. Finding the suitcase, he pulled it out and straightened. "Okay, then, what do you need?"

They spent some time going through what she might need for a night or two, then he zipped the suitcase shut and took it to her door.

Macy followed, slowly. She didn't recognize this, the caring, protective attitude. She bristled. Who did he think he was, coming in and … taking care of her. Oh. Then she felt the flutterbies again, along with a profound loneliness. Amy and her brother knew what had happened, and they hadn't been concerned. It probably wasn't real to them, or they hadn't recognized that she needed them. Macy really couldn't fault them for that; it was a chicken-and-egg thing. She'd had to invite herself to spend the night at the house after going out with Amy. Either they hadn't made the connection, or they thought it was business as usual for competent, badass Macy.

Thomas, for his part, was trying not to show his anxiety too much. Death was too close to her. Taking charge wasn't new to him, but feeling responsible, protective, was. He was the third son, with a baby sister after him, with whom he had always been close but never an authority figure. In her own way, Macy had become his. Maybe because she took care of other people but wasn't taken care of herself; maybe because he didn't have anyone else to take care of, but there it was. She was his.

She stopped him at the door. "You don't have to do this."

He looked down at her, taking her bag. "If I felt I had to do it, I wouldn't be so inclined. I want to do this. End of story. You good?"

Macy surveyed her apartment before nodding, then they went into the hallway and she locked the door behind her.

Together they went down the hall.

Once they reached his place, he immediately placed her overnight bag in his bedroom as she stood in the foyer, taking off her jacket and shoes. After dropping off her bag, he joined her. Thomas kissed her lightly and hugged her, wrapping his arms around her and pulling her close.

"Thank you," Macy mumbled into his chest. Thomas chuckled and released her.

"Can I get you anything?" He asked, walking into the kitchen. "Are you hungry? Thirsty?"

Macy just shook her head no from where she was leaning against the doorframe.

"Sure I can't tempt you?"

Thomas laughed at the cocked eyebrow he got in response. He walked back to her, resting his arms on the doorframe around her. He leaned down and kissed her, a light one, followed by a little nibble.

Macy inched up on tiptoe to kiss him back, sliding her hands onto his chest to steady herself. Soon, though, the kiss deepened; her knees grew weak and she moved her hands to his back for a better grip. Thomas dropped his arms to her sides, running his hands up and down before wrapping one in her hair. The other moved to her bottom and pulled her even closer. He staggered back a little, until he was braced against the counter. Macy stretched along him until he suddenly picked her up, wrapping her legs around him and twirling around, sat her down on the counter.

Now that his hands were free, Thomas set them to her shirt, pulling it up and over her head. As he kissed her neck from the earlobe down, Macy's hands went to his shirt, unbuttoning it in a very distracted, impatient manner. She gasped as the air hit her skin when he slid her bra off, then gasped again when his mouth progressed from her neck to her breast. Her reach compromised, she resorted to tugging his shirt off one jerky movement at a time, until he assisted with the cuffs and let it drop to the floor. While his hands were behind him, fighting with the cuffs, she slid off the counter, turned him around so he was against it again. Then her lips went to work.

She started at his ear, tracing it with her tongue and nibbling the earlobe with a swift bite that made him groan. She let her tongue flicker down his neck to his chest as her fingernails traced lightly on his skin.

She almost sighed when she got to his abs, and he did sigh when her tongue traced his treasure trail to his beltline. Her hands got his belt off as he gripped the counter edge tightly. She popped his pants button then slowly slid them down over his hips. Macy outlined his boxer briefs with her tongue as he stepped out of his pants, hooking a finger into each sock to remove them too.

Thomas took her arms to pull her up to face him. His eyelids were heavy, his pupils wide. "Wait here. Don't move," he said in a low voice, before repeating, "Don't move."

He strode out of the kitchen in his boxer briefs, the muscles in his butt and thighs working nicely to Macy's view. She hugged herself for a moment, topless. In a flash Thomas was back from his bedroom, a square foil packet in hand. He set the condom on the counter to the side, then turned back to Macy.

He kissed her again, hard, as he undid her pants and dropped them. Instead of bending he picked her up, out of them, and put her back on the counter, still kissing her. While one hand played with the elastic around her panties, the other gently pushed her back, so she was reclining on her elbows.

Thomas kissed her chin, the hollow at the base of her throat, the space between her breasts. He let his tongue slip from her navel to her panties before his hands slid them off and his tongue slid further.

Soon her back was arching and her hands were flying, reaching for him. She hooked her toes in the waistband of his boxer briefs and tried to work them down, until he helped her out by removing them himself.

When they were both naked he stood up straight and looked at her. "Macy," he said. She tried to match his seriousness with "Thomas," and they both smiled. Then she handed him the condom.

He tore open the packet and slid the condom on, then held onto the counter as she inched closer to the edge. She exhaled slowly, softly, as he entered.

They were close enough for her arms to reach around him, allowing her to let her fingernails graze his back. Her heels rested on his butt, guiding. Their eyes kept flitting open and closed, they searched greedily for each other's mouths. They were losing breath as the pace intensified, then suddenly Thomas stilled.

He looked at her again, held her and slid her off the counter, wrapping her legs around him. Not breaking contact, he braced himself by widening his stance and bending his knees slightly, then he started slowly sliding her up and down. It would occur to Macy later that he had some serious strength to hold the position, but at the moment she just enjoyed. They both did, for several moments longer.

CHAPTER NINETEEN

A couple days later, Macy headed to Derek's before the drop. Thomas would join them for a little celebration after the money was scheduled to be picked up. The atmosphere was casual and relaxed. Vaughn sat smoking his pipe in his chair. Anabelle was playing with her toys. Joshua and Derek got up to go at the appointed hour, but Derek stopped when Macy made no move to join them.

"Aren't you coming?"

She waved them on. "You don't need me anymore. Just make sure you get everything, all the pages."

He gave her an unusual look, then turned quickly and let the door slam shut behind him. Startled, Macy turned to Amy. "What's with him?"

Amy shrugged. "Got me. He's been in a bad mood today, when he should be happy this is over."

"Speaking of happy endings…" Macy looked at Vaughn. "Ah, Anabelle, could you give us some grown-up time, please?"

After a little protesting Anabelle went to her room and Macy spoke directly to Vaughn.

"So. You and Grandma, eh?"

He was so startled he choked on his pipe. After the ensuing coughing fit, he said, "I don't know what you're talking about."

Macy smiled. Amy listened intently.

"I read her diary, Vaughn."

"Her diary?"

She nodded. "That's what this was all about. Vincent obviously poked around my place when I wasn't there, or when I wasn't looking. He found her diary and found out about the priest. But you were … um, shall we say, mentioned often. And with much affection." Her tone was heavy with implied teasing.

Vaughn paled, then slowly started turning pink. "I was? What did she say? Did she… How did she feel… I, I didn't know there was a diary…"

"It was in my mom's things. I guess she got it after Grandma died."

Vaughn nodded. "She did most of the work when Libby died. Your father was too upset."

Macy snorted softly. "Doesn't surprise me."

"So, ah…"

Macy smiled kindly at him. "Grandma loved you. You loved her, too, didn't you?"

The old man nodded without hesitation. "I did."

"Okay wait! Hold the phone!" Amy interrupted as the pieces clicked together. "Macy, you saying that Vaughn and your Grandma hooked up or somethin'?" She looked shocked.

With a laugh Macy nodded emphatically. "Oh yeah, baby! That's what I'm saying!"

"Shut the front door!" Amy exclaimed. Vaughn turned even more red.

"We did not hook up, young lady. We had ah, um, a very civilized love affair." He sat back in his chair, his pipe forgotten in his fingers. "I never told no one."

"Why didn't she leave Grandpa for you? So you could be together?"

Vaughn shook his head. "Your Grandpa was my best friend, and my cousin. He wasn't right after the war. Your Grandma and me, we weren't proud of it, but we couldn't stop."

Macy digested this. It was Amy who went there first. "So, Mace, your dad... Vaughn, are you ... is their dad...?"

Vaughn shrugged, then remembered his pipe and stuck it in his mouth. Macy's eyes went wide and she sat back. Again it was Amy who spoke next.

"Does Derek know? That why he's in a bad mood?"

Macy replied, "He knows about the affair. I gave him the diary to read but he said it creeped him out, thinking of Grandma like that. Don't know if he's made the connection about Dad yet."

Macy caught the look on Amy's face. "It doesn't change much, you know."

Amy shook her head. "I know, it's just, that's the first time you've mentioned your dad in years. Not since your mom died."

Again, Macy was unsettled. Then Anabelle called from upstairs, asking if she could come down and join them, which she did. Macy hugged her for an extra-long time.

Thomas had already arrived by the time Derek and Joshua returned, later than expected. They entered silently, with serious looks on their faces. They flopped into seats in the living room, Joshua rubbing his face with both hands and Derek just looking straight ahead, shaking his head.

"What happened?" Macy asked in a worried tone.

"Didn't show. All that, and the little rat bastard ain't home," Derek said.

"Not a sign of him, either. We waited. We checked his work, his gym, went back to his place again. Nada," Joshua added.

"Did you go inside his place?"

Joshua turned to Derek. "Told you she'd ask."

"Yeah, yeah. Went inside but ain't nothing there. He cleared out. His clothes, his car, gone. Left in a hurry too."

Thomas and Macy exchanged looks beside each other on the couch, then he asked, "Did you look for any extra pages?"

Derek nodded. "Couldn't find 'em, though. Maybe he didn't copy the whole thing, just the beginning."

Thomas took a deep breath, rolled his shoulders and sat back. "He's running."

"With the diary entries we need."

"But they show it was the mob who killed the priest, not Vaughn or your grandmother."

"Which means he can't hurt us by taking them to the police."

"But it does mean…"

Thomas and Macy looked at each other again. "Uh oh," she said.

"You think?"

"Don't know! Could be."

Everyone else had watched the exchange in silence. Amy finally burst, "Hey, what's going on?"

Macy turned to her. "The diary entries show Vaughn and Grandma and Grandpa didn't kill the priest, but they do show who did — mobsters. They show there were witnesses. And Vaughn's still alive, and he was a witness to a mob hit, and the mob might be interested to know there's a witness still around."

"Okay, so we don't got to worry about the cops, but we gotta worry about the mob instead?" Derek asked.

Joshua added, "Well, there were those guys who got to him before we did, Derek, when we went over."

Thomas shook his head. "No, those were my people."

Macy turned to him. "You have people?"

Thomas shrugged. "What's important is, does Vincent have people with mob connections?"

Macy straightened. "Uh oh."

"What?"

"Vincent's people."

"Vincent got people too? I'm confused." Derek's face showed it.

"No, Vincent's people. His family. I think … but I don't know. I mean, nothing definite…" Little things began sliding into place for Macy. "I think Vincent might be more connected than we thought."

"What makes you say that?" Thomas shifted on the couch so he could look at her straight on.

"He wouldn't talk about his family, wouldn't introduce me, even when we started talking about wedding plans. I don't know what, but there's something there. He definitely wanted to keep it hidden. I don't know how far it goes, though."

Everyone paused for a moment, then Thomas jumped in. "Okay, so Vincent is running, with our evidence, and he may or may not be able to sell the secret to someone with an interest in a murder that happened last century."

He stood. "I'm going to find him."

"How?" Macy stood as well. "Your people?"

Thomas looked at her softly. "I'll explain soon, I promise. Let's just deal with Vincent first, okay?"

Macy hesitated a moment to show her displeasure at his secrets and his methods. "Alright."

"Alright. I've got a call to make."

"To your people?" Macy's tone told everyone she wasn't happy. Thomas stopped, then pulled her into the hallway with him.

"Don't worry, Macy. We'll fix this." He hugged her.

"And then you'll tell me about your people?" Macy's words were a little muffled, as she was speaking them into his chest in the middle of his embrace. He chuckled.

"Yes. I'll tell you everything and anything you want to know. Later." He bent and kissed her, then stepped onto the veranda to make his call. Macy shut the door and returned to the living room.

Thomas rejoined them a few minutes later as everyone sat around chatting. He nodded at Macy to reassure her. They were speculating on what might happen next, but even considering the new development Derek's mood was odd. Macy gestured to him to join her in the kitchen away from everyone else. Once there she sat in a chair, expecting him to do the same, but he leaned against the sink, away from her.

"I talked to Vaughn. He admitted it, said he and Grandma were in love and had a love affair."

"Whoa."

"Do you think, maybe, Vaughn could be our grandfather?"

Derek considered it for a moment, then shrugged. "Don't matter much. He's always been part of the family."

Macy nodded in agreement. "Well, I guess that's that. Mystery solved, crisis over." She stood to return to the living room. Derek stayed where he was, crossing his arms over his chest.

"So I guess that's it, then. You gonna disappear again, pretend we're not alive."

"What?" Macy was startled into stopping.

Derek snorted. "You heard me."

"Is that what's got you in such a bad mood?"

"Whatever. You have a nice life, sis."

"Derek, I…"

"He's getting out soon, you know that? Next year or two, depending on parole. He's almost done his time."

"Dad?" Two mentions in one day, after years of not acknowledging him at all, registered on Macy. "I didn't know that."

"No, you didn't. You never even went to see him in the joint. He didn't die like Mom did, you know."

Now Macy was getting defensive. "No, he didn't. And while he was in jail, she did."

"Oh, so what, now you're blaming him for Mom dying?"

"He should've been there for her!"

"What would you know about being there!"

Macy was aware of a hush in the living room, then the music was turned up. She stepped closer to Derek, her hands on her hips. "What's your point, Derek? What's going on?"

He scowled at her before continuing. "You wanna know what my point is? Fine. You come back and you save the day and now you're just gonna disappear again. Joshua and Amy are getting married soon, then they're gonna move out. Vaughn might change his mind and go back to the nursing home then. Mom's dead and Dad's in the joint and…"

Macy dropped her hands and stepped closer to him. "And you'll be alone? Is that what you're afraid of?"

Derek looked up at the ceiling and blinked several times. Macy put her hand on his arm.

"I've been alone for years, Derek."

"That was your choice. You was the one ashamed of us. Sometimes, I guess, I can't blame you for that. I didn't know it was hard for you to get work, or about you getting dumped and stuff."

"You're right." She paused and took a deep breath. "Look, I can't promise anything about Dad. You have a relationship with him and that's great! But I need you to stop pressuring me to have one too. If it happens, it happens, and it has nothing to do with you. I know you want the family to be together but… I just, I just don't know. But I can try. With you."

Derek swooped her into his arms in a big hug. "Just don't wanna lose you again, sis. You is my family."

Now Macy was welling up. After a moment she muttered, "Well, actually, we just got a new Grandpa in the next room."

That made them both chuckle. They straightened and stepped away, both brushing their cheeks.

"You're such a sissy!" Macy teased him.

"Shut up!" Derek gave her a light push.

After sorting themselves, they went back into the living room, where everyone ignored their fight, and soon the group disbanded. At her request, Thomas drove Macy back to his place to pick up her things, then took her home. As they walked into her apartment Thomas asked, "So, you and Derek okay?"

She nodded. "I don't know what'll happen now that this is over, but I guess he wants me around somehow."

"And you? What do you want?"

He said it casually but it knocked her flat. She really didn't know. Macy had lived a certain way for a long time, devoted her energy to avoiding her family, her past and the remnants that survived in her. "Good question."

She flopped onto the couch and tried to catch her breath. She was horrified to find tears in her eyes, then got up quickly to dash to the bathroom, mumbling about excusing herself before he could notice.

He stopped her on the way, catching her elbow. "Hey, what's wrong? I'm sorry. We don't have to talk about it."

"I'm just, ah, I'm fine."

He looked at her. "Of course you are. That's you, that's what you're about. You're always fine, aren't you?"

She blinked hard but still wouldn't look at him. "What's that supposed to mean?"

Thomas paused. "I just... It's okay to need people, you know. To want them in your life."

"Are you talking about Derek or you?"

Now it was his turn to reflect. Macy continued to the bathroom as he took a place on the couch. When she returned she sat next to him.

"You know, I'm not the only enigma around here." She was fully aware she had slipped into defensive mode but just couldn't help it. She took a deep breath and tried to be reasonable, to see it from his point of view like she had tried with Derek.

"Are you concerned we might be over once the mystery's solved and the case is closed?"

Thomas chuckled. "Yes, I suppose that's it." He draped an arm over the leg she had tucked up onto the couch.

"Well, I hadn't planned to get rid of you." Yes, she was blunt. "Were you planning on getting rid of me?"

"No. Not at all."

"Well, okay then. But you know, I still don't know much about you at all."

When he didn't immediately reply, she continued. "You smell too good for my old neighbourhood. You're obviously slumming but trying not to be obvious. Personally, I'm kinda hoping you're a cop, not a crook, but I don't know what you want with my family, since you showed up before the blackmailing began."

That made him laugh. "I'm not a cop. Or a crook, for that matter."

"Oh. Well. In that case, do you want something to drink?"

They wandered into her kitchen. "Hey, what about this?" He picked up a bottle of wine from the rack by the door that separated the kitchen and dining room.

"Okay then." She shut the fridge door and reached into a nearby drawer. She flung the corkscrew to him and took two glasses from her shelf. "I'll probably need that if we're going to play twenty questions."

They went back to the couch where Thomas filled their glasses. They talked well into the night, with barely any mention of family and just a little bit about the future.

July 2, 1952

Dear Diary,

Vaughn's coming home! I got a postcard from Germany — he's on his way!

CHAPTER TWENTY

Macy rolled over in her bed the next morning to find Thomas already dressed, sitting on the edge of the bed and leaning in towards her. He stopped when she woke up, smiled and said, "Good morning."

She smile and stretched. "Morning. You leaving?"

He nodded. "Got a message from my people saying they may have some news on Vincent. I have to go. But I'll see you later?" He gently moved a lock of her hair away so he could see her face.

She covered a yawn while nodding. "I'm helping Amy with some wedding stuff today, so I may be over there for a bit."

"Okay," Thomas smiled at her. "I have to say, I like the image you're leaving me with."

"You perv." They both laughed. She was naked under the sheets, as he had been until he got up that morning. He leaned over and kissed her goodbye, lingering a few moments before tearing himself away. She heard him leave, then she got up, grabbed a robe, walked to her door and locked it behind him. Then she turned into the kitchen and started the coffee maker before making her way to the bathroom.

She stood under the spray of a hot shower for a few minutes, thinking about the delicious minutes she'd had with Thomas, savouring them, smiling. She didn't know what was going to happen once Vincent was taken care of, but she did hope she'd have more time with Thomas. More minutes and moments.

She was rinsing conditioner out when it struck her. He still hadn't told her about his background, why or how he had people, and yet it didn't seem that important anymore. He was in her life, and she didn't know how that came to be, but she liked it. She wanted him in her life, regardless of how he got there.

Macy recalled hearing a joke about how falling in love killed IQ points. She wondered where her brain was when the rest of her was busy ... should she even go there? So soon?

She shut off the water and grabbed her towel. *Oh Thomas*, she thought as she wrapped it around herself. *Please don't be a bad guy.*

She was considering her new perspective as she stepped into the hallway and walked to her bedroom. So she was a little preoccupied and didn't notice the man with the knife until he grabbed her from behind and held it to her throat.

***

Macy watched Vincent pace back and forth. They were on the roof of her apartment building, about an hour after he grabbed her in her bedroom. She had convinced him to at least let her get dressed, reasoning with him that a woman in a towel would attract more attention. She dressed in her usual riding outfit, including the boots. Mentally she was preparing the missing persons alert: Macy Carruthers, last seen wearing three-inch ass-kicking boots... At least she'd go out in style. He led her to the roof, muttering about needing space, a place to think. Every now and then as he turned, she caught a glimpse of papers sticking slightly out of his back pants pocket. She was fairly certain she had found the missing diary entries. Or rather, they had found her.

It was sunny but windy this far up, and she sat with her back against a wall for shelter. Vincent paced, muttering to himself, his hands gesturing sporadically. Macy had covered a few laps of the roof's perimeter herself before choosing a spot and sitting down. The roofs of the neighbouring buildings were really close, but very empty when they arrived. "Vincent, calm down. What's going on? You got me up here. You may as well tell me."

He looked up from the cell phone he was compulsively checking every few minutes. "Hmm? What?"

Macy stretched her legs out to get more comfortable, then moved them beneath her so she was kneeling. It was hard on the concrete, but the door was just a few feet away, and if she sprung while he was distracted... "I said, why don't you tell me why you brought me up here? Actually, why don't you start by telling me how you got into my apartment again."

Vincent stopped pacing and looked at her, despair on his face. "Your building guy..."

"Mr. Lee?"

Vincent nodded, swallowed. Macy rose to stand. "So that was you! You killed Mr. Lee!"

That agitated him again and his pacing resumed. "I didn't mean to, I swear it, Macy! It's just, he saw me, I had gone back to your apartment but you changed the lock and I couldn't get in, then I was leaving and he saw me and he started yelling, telling me to get out, he was going to call the police if I bothered you again. He went for his phone and I just panicked. The kick was instinct."

"Muscle memory? Like you taught in class at the gym?"

He nodded. "Like I taught in class at the gym."

It was surreal, hearing that someone she had once loved had taken a man's life. She swallowed. "You got my new key…"

He nodded again. "The new one was pretty obvious on his key chain. Shiny. Stood out. I… When I kicked him, he just flew through the door and down the stairs! I froze, but no one was around. I went down to check and he, and his neck…" He looked away for a moment. "But his keys were there, they were right there, so I grabbed the one I thought was yours and I ran."

"What about the nursing home? Was that you too? Did you kill Victor too?"

"That was an accident! I went there to leave the note for Vaughn, but the room wasn't empty, that other guy was there. He surprised me. I pushed him out of the way to leave and he fell. Hit his head against the corner of the bed frame. At first I went to call for help, get a nurse or something, but I had just dropped off the first note…"

Macy was stunned, but tried to calm her mind enough to be aware of her surroundings. When Vincent looked away from her and back down at the ground as he paced, she inched closer to the door.

Unfortunately, he was also aware. He jerked to a stop and came at her, dagger in hand. He grabbed her arm and dragged her further away from the door. "I'm sorry, Macy, you're not going anywhere. Not until that boyfriend of yours gives me my money."

"What? But he already gave you money. You could've gotten away by now."

"Not enough, not enough. Macy, I'm in deep this time. I screwed up. And I don't know how I'm going to get out if I don't get away."

Against her fear instinct, she turned towards him this time. "Vincent, I can't help if I don't know what's going on. Tell me." She put her hand on his arm, speaking in a soft, low voice. The voice of someone he could trust, someone he didn't have to fear — or watch so closely. He released her and slumped against the wall.

"You can't help me, Macy."

"At least tell me what this is about. C'mon, Vincent, talk to me."

He looked at her, desperation shining on his sweating face. He took a big breath and blurted it out. "A family connection gave me a tip about a new IPO. I passed it on to some clients; it went big. They wanted more, so I moved more of their money into it. But it was bogus. The whole thing was shut down a few weeks ago during that big drug bust. Turns out it was just a front: The whole company was just part of a money laundering operation for drug dealers."

"Go on."

"It's bad enough I passed on the tip from some inside information. If I can't cover the losses, they'll find out I'm connected and it'll tie me into the whole operation. But I swear, Macy, I swear I didn't know. I thought it was legit. I should've known, though."

Suddenly he turned and slammed his fist against the wall, startling her. "Damn it!"

"Who gave you the tip, Vincent?"

He didn't look at her, just leaned with his fist on the wall looking down at the concrete. "One of my uncles. Said he was trying to mend fences. Said he was proud of me, said he wanted to show I didn't need to be ashamed of them anymore."

Macy desperately tried to remember the news about the drug bust. Suddenly the headline from the old newspaper in the nursing-home lobby came to mind. "This uncle…"

Vincent nodded. "He was caught in the bust. So I can't tell work what happened, I can't tell the police, I can't tell anyone. I have no way out, Macy."

She paused, sensing the seal was broken. Sure enough, he continued. "You, you have no idea how much money there is! How it flows. How hard it is to figure out what to do with it. Think about it. You have a deal here, a deal there, wholesale or bulk, you're talking tens of thousands of dollars in cash. Where do you keep it? The sheer physical space it takes up… But how do you buy anything with a box full of money? How do you buy a car these days, or a house? No, you need a credit history, but anything in a bank over ten grand gets flagged. Terrorists! You could be a terrorist, so the bank tells the government. So you set something up, hope it works well enough or long enough before the laws catch up. Then the financial types start acting like mob bosses themselves, moving some here, breaking rules there."

Now he was mumbling and shouting as he paced. "Then everybody gets greedy. Yeah, everybody. I got greedy. Do you know what it's like, growing up, surrounded by all that, all that money? Not having any yourself? Everybody else, always getting the best clothes, the best toys, the best trips. You have to work twice as hard to get half as good. And you're tainted. All the teachers think you're one of them, so they treat you like it's your photo in the paper after the latest bust. So screw them, screw them all, you figure, you can do it on your own. You grow up, you get far, but you can never get far enough."

He stopped and stared at her, not really seeing while he fiddled with the knife. "And you realize, you can't do it. Not on your own. Because everyone is connected, really. In one way or another, everyone is connected."

Vincent started pacing again. "Old money, even legit, it opens doors. The proper name, the right school... Like your boyfriend." He laughed and pointed at her. "You went from me to him. You think he's going to take you, with your background? At least I make a lot of money, I can get the women... But you. You were too..."

He went back to muttering and looking down. "You were too smart. You would've figured me out."

"Oh, Vincent." Macy reached out to pat his arm but he jerked it away — wisely on his part, since she was actually aiming for the knife. "You could've told me, Vincent. We would've figured it out."

He snorted. "After how I dumped you? Why would you help me?"

That made her pause. She removed her hand and leaned against the wall herself, pulling her helping instinct into check.

"What was that all about, anyway?"

He chuckled and shook his head. "I'm just one big screw-up. You're too smart. You were getting too close. You would've figured out sooner or later that I'm just a fraud."

"You could've trusted me, you know."

Vincent looked at her then. "I did trust you. I just... I didn't think you'd trust me if you knew, if you knew about my family." He chuckled again. "I found your grandmother's diary when I was trying to find out more about you, you know. You're not exactly Miss Transparency either."

"You shouldn't have snuck around like that, Vincent."

"Oh, Macy, get real. That's the least of my sins by now."

She blinked, took a breath. His sins now included two murders, even if they were just manslaughter as he claimed. "So. What happens now? What's the plan?"

As he opened his mouth to respond, the door to the roof opened suddenly and Thomas rushed out. Vincent gave a start, then grabbed Macy again, putting her in front of himself and bringing the dagger back to her throat. Thomas immediately stopped and put his hands up.

"Stop right there, lover boy," Vincent snapped at him. "Don't move!"

"Okay, okay, whoa, calm down. No one needs to get hurt here," Thomas said.

Macy's left hand was on the arm Vincent had around her, while her right was on the arm that held the knife up. Instinctively she tried to angle her neck away from the blade. "Thomas! How did you find me?"

"Amy called. She knew something was wrong when you didn't show up and didn't answer your phone. Then I got a message demanding more money or he'd hurt you." Thomas wasn't taking his eyes off Vincent and the knife.

"How did you know where to find me?"

"Your cell phone is still in your apartment, but the guy I've had watching you said you hadn't left the building. So it was just a matter of finding you in the building."

"What guy watching me? You had someone watching me?!"

"Maybe this isn't the best time to discuss that…"

Both of Macy's hands now flew to her hips and she almost stomped her foot. She moved with enough force that Vincent had to move to a new angle behind her. "When is it a good time, Thomas? Before or after I get my throat slit by someone else who lied to cover his ass?"

Macy leaned back and Vincent had to shuffle back a step to take her weight. Thomas took a small step forward, and in return they took a step backward, closer to the edge of the building.

"Ah, man, don't piss her off," Vincent said as he noticed how close they were to the edge. His stress was showing in his strained voice that sounded higher and louder than normal.

"Well, Macy, seeing as how you're being blackmailed and there were two murders and your apartment was broken into, I got a little ... concerned."

"So you had your people follow me?"

"Think of it more like, oh, a guardian angel. And it was just my bodyguard, Woodley, when I couldn't be with you. He's become rather fond of you, you know. He'd like to keep you alive too."

"Listen, mister," Macy shifted again and Vincent had to adjust. "We are going to have a serious talk about personal boundaries once we're out of here."

Vincent shifted again. "Enough chit chat. Where's my money?"

Thomas raised his hands again. "It's downstairs, in Macy's apartment."

"Why didn't you bring it up here?"

"I couldn't be sure you were really up here. And I had to see if she was okay."

Vincent seemed to accept this. "Fine. I'm going to leave you both up here. I'm going to take the money, and I'm going to keep the notes from the diary. If you come after me, I'll hand the notes over to people who really don't like leaving witnesses behind."

"Your family, you mean? Your people?" Macy's hands were back on Vincent's arms.

"They had nothing to do with that priest, but they know people who'd find the information valuable."

"I'm really beginning to hate people's people."

"Alright. You," Vincent jerked his head towards Thomas and gestured to the side of the building. "Stand over there. Now." Thomas obliged, moving out of the way to give Vincent a clear path to the roof's door. Letting him go didn't matter, as long as Macy was safe. Macy mattered, really mattered, to Thomas.

"Hey, Vincent?"

"What now, Macy?"

"Remember that time in class at the gym when you talked about not telegraphing your next move?" Suddenly Macy grabbed his knife hand, brought it to her mouth and bit down hard. Vincent yelled and dropped the knife. She then used her heavy heeled boots to stomp down on his instep, while throwing her head back and smashing his nose. Her elbow to his solar plexus gave her the distance she needed to break his grasp. He let go of her, and as she whirled around she grabbed the pages from his back pocket, throwing them behind her towards Thomas.

Vincent was teetering on the edge of the roof when she heard a sharp *pop, pop*, and red appeared on his chest. Arms spread out and whirling, he fell backwards, seemingly in slow motion but too fast to believe, falling over the edge and out of her sight.

Macy was stunned. She turned to Thomas, who was suddenly holding a gun in his hands, and cried loudly, "You shot him!"

"I didn't," he said, bringing his arms down and tucking the gun into his waistband behind him. "They did." He reached her in a few steps, and as he hugged her, he gestured to the roofs on either side of the building. Macy looked, and saw Derek on one, Joshua on the other. It was hard to tell what they were holding, but it looked like guns. Really big plastic guns. In neon colours. Both men waved at her.

"They shot him with paintball guns?"

Thomas shrugged. "We didn't have a lot of time. We had to improvise."

"But your gun is real?"

He nodded.

"You brought a gun to a paintball fight?"

"Never mind about that. Are you okay?" Thomas tried examining her throat, running his hands over her as though to check her physical condition. "Did he hurt you?"

"I'm fine, really. Thomas, please. I need to know. Why do you have a real gun?"

He stopped and looked at her. Ah, hell, he was tired of not being straight with her. "Macy, I've had a couple ... kidnapping threats against me." He said it so nonchalantly it irritated her.

"What? Why on earth would someone want to kidnap you?"

"Threats against my family aren't that ... uncommon. So I have a real gun. And sometimes a bodyguard, like Woodley. And some people who know some people."

"Oh."

"Um, Macy? Stay here, okay? I just need to see if..."

Thomas stepped away from her and towards the edge, where Vincent fell.

"If we killed him?" Macy finished his thought. "Nope. I was making a fuss for a purpose, you know. I picked the spot to push him over."

Sure enough, when Thomas peered over, there was Vincent, lying on a fire escape a floor down, groaning.

Thomas recognized he felt indifference rather than relief. The man had held a knife to Macy's throat, had put her in harm's way and had caused her pain. He had killed at least two people and had threatened her. Damn straight Thomas would have used the real gun, as Macy put it. He would have used the weapon and the years of training he had to go with it. He turned back to her, caught her in another hug and gave her a kiss that showed how scared he had been at the thought of losing her.

By the time they came up for air, Joshua and Derek had gotten to Vincent on the fire escape and were getting the bruised blackmailer to his feet after tying his hands behind his back.

Thomas and Macy looked down at them from where they stood still holding each other. "Hey guys, thanks!"

"Anytime, sis! It's nice being the good guys for once," Derek grinned at her, making her smile in return.

"Hey Mace, you might want to give Amy a call. She's freaking out with worry," Joshua called up.

Thomas pulled her back. "You can call later," he murmured, then kissed her again.

She really should call Amy, Macy thought. And she would be good and responsible and do that. In a minute. In a few delicious minutes. She kissed him right back.

CHAPTER TWENTY-ONE

A couple of days later, after Joshua and Derek had bundled up Vincent and put him where police would find him and left an anonymous tip to check his work accounts, Thomas picked Macy up at her apartment. She was just getting off the phone with a very worried Ellie, calling from several time zones away about the email Macy had sent just after Mr. Lee was killed. She had been trying to call Macy ever since, but Macy had spent some time with Thomas with her cell phone turned off and forgotten. Quite a bit of time, actually.

Macy was glad she could report it had all worked out in the end. She had to repeat it several times to convince her friend to not take the next flight home. Macy was still smiling from her conversation when she got into Thomas's car. She kissed him hello, then snapped his photo with her phone.

"Sorry, had to do that." She sent the photo to Ellie, fulfilling the promise she had made to make up for the panic she had caused. It was nice to be loved, from near and far. Some connections were always there, she thought, also thinking about Amy, Derek and Joshua. Maybe she wasn't as alone as she thought after all.

"Where are we going?" she asked after putting her phone away and turning back to Thomas.

"You'll see," he answered and started driving.

"Yeah, cause that's going to cut it with me." Macy stared at him until he broke.

"I want to show you where I work."

"Oh. Okay. See, was that hard to tell me?" Macy teased.

Thomas shook his head no, thinking of how to tell her the rest. Soon they were in front of the high-rise office building downtown. He pulled into his parking spot in the lot, the one with his full name on the reserved sign. He noticed Macy noticing it, but she was quiet.

He unbuckled his seat belt after turning the car off. Thomas took a deep breath, then turned to his right to look at her.

"Well, this is it. This is where I work. The family business."

Macy nodded silently. Another deep breath, then he poured it out.

"Please don't be upset, I didn't mean to lie or keep things from you or anything like that... Grandfather asked me to help Vaughn, only I didn't know it was Vaughn at the time, he just said it was an old friend from when he was a kid. And I really did meet your brother in jail, so I already knew him. It was my kid sister, wild party, stupid story. It was just before they legalized pot. But anyway. In Vaughn's story, you know the friend from Montreal? The one who was in the back of the truck when they all saw the priest get shot? That was my grandfather. He started the brewery when they all moved to Toronto. There were always rumours about how he got started, but he's always been very careful about avoiding personal publicity. Now I understand why. So um, yeah, I'm ah, I guess you could say, I'm, well, not just me, per se, but the family, we're ah…"

"Rich? Rich enough to have kidnapping threats against you since you were a kid? Filthy stinking rich?"

He blinked. "Yes, I guess you could say that."

Slowly Macy smiled. She reached out to touch his hand. "I know," she said matter-of-factly.

"What?"

She looked at him. "You really think I didn't learn my lesson with Vincent? I ran a background check on you."

"You ran a background check on me?"

She nodded. "You can't get mad at me, either. You met my brother in jail. I needed to know where the money came from. I needed to make sure we weren't getting into something even worse than blackmail. You have to admit, the gun, the bodyguard, the threats against your family… If I didn't know better, I would've thought you were in the mob yourself."

That made sense. "Oh."

"The good news is I've made a new friend at work. Turns out Tracey is totally cool with digging up background on men. The point is, though, I didn't want to rush you or anything. Let's focus on that."

"Huh."

"Besides, it's not like you could hide it that well. The gala had your last name splashed everywhere. Then Vincent's date, your brother and sister-in-law… The car! And, by the way, the really big sign in front of this building that we passed as we drove into the parking lot."

"Oh."

"But thank you for your help. And for caring about lying… I'm not entirely sure, but thanks. I think."

"You're welcome. So you're not mad?"

"Nope. Are you?"

"About the background check?"

"Yup."

"Nope."

"So we're good?"

"I think so. I think we're very good." He leaned forward and kissed her. "Oh, just one more thing."

"Uh oh."

"Grandfather wants to meet you. Right now." Thomas slipped out of the car even as Macy was still exclaiming, "What?"

He raced around the car to open her door and get her out of her seat. He took her by the hand and led her out, then shut the door and clicked his key fob to lock it. He held her hand as he led the way into the building. "Um, Thomas? You didn't tell me I'd be meeting your family!"

"Well, technically you've already met some of them, at the gala. You'll be fine, really. Grandfather's terrific."

"But am I dressed okay? Should I have brought something? Why are we meeting him at the office?"

Thomas stopped and looked at her. "You look great, you always do. Of course not. And I'm not sure, but he does still spend a lot of time at work." He resumed his not-quite dragging but more determined leading.

They entered the large lobby and Thomas waved them past security. Macy glanced at the directory on the wall to see if she could spot his name, but they were into an elevator in a flash. Thomas hit the button for the top floor. He was still holding her hand, and he rocked back and forth on his feet a little in his impatience. He wore a small smile but didn't know it. His confession had worked out better than he expected, which made him happy. He should have known she'd catch on. He was just glad she wasn't mad.

"So, that background check?" he started.

"Mmm-hmm?" Macy was distracted by the sense of impending doom that accompanied the situation. She was about to meet his grandfather, the head honcho, the other player in the mystery, and, most importantly, Thomas was introducing her to his family. *Well, more of his family*, she thought, remembering the gala.

"What else did you find out about me?"

She grinned. "I'll never tell."

"Never?"

"Well. Maybe in my diary." She gave him a wink. The elevator doors opened and they stepped off. There was only one office on this floor, and there were two large doors to pass through to enter. Thomas started opening one of them, then stopped.

"You keep a diary?"

Macy laughed. Thomas opened the door and they strode through. An older lady sat at a wide desk. Macy got the feeling this was the place where the buck stopped.

"Thomas, good to see you."

"Hello, Miss Eleanor. Grandfather's expecting me."

"I know. And is this Miss Carruthers?"

Thomas did the introductions and Macy said, "Pleased to meet you." She was given a friendly smile and a "Likewise, my dear," in return, then Eleanor said, "You can go right in."

They stepped beyond the desk and went through the doorway behind it, into the actual office. It was huge. Aside from the heavy old-fashioned desk in the corner by the wall-to-wall windows, there was a sitting area with a liquor cabinet, two chairs, a coffee table and a couch.

Vaughn was sitting in one of the chairs, a drink in his hand, a cigar in the other.

A man of a similar age rose from his chair to greet them. "Thomas! You're here! And this must be Macy."

"Hello! Pleased to meet you, sir." Macy offered her hand to shake but he bent and kissed it instead.

"Sir! Bah! I'm not old enough to be sir! You call me John. And you come sit down next to me, young lady." He sat down on the couch and indicated the space next to him. "Thomas! Get this girl a drink! Don't keep a lady waiting."

Macy laughed and sat. Thomas dutifully turned to the liquor cabinet and started rummaging.

"Hi, Vaughn!" Macy said, shooting him a look. "Didn't expect to see you here."

He waved at her with his cigar. "Just shooting the breeze with an old friend here. Lots to catch up on."

"So it's true, then," Thomas said, pulling out various bottles for Macy to yay or nay with a shake of her head. "The two of you were part of the gang back then. Grandfather, you bingo rascal!" He mouthed "Martini?" to Macy who shrugged her approval. She was more of a wine girl, but she supposed a martini in an office penthouse would have to do. Especially when visiting with two men who had been on the run from the mob for decades.

The drink was barely in her hand before the door opened again and a very solid-looking man walked in carrying a folder. His suit was more a uniform of some sort, so Macy assumed he was security.

"Walter! What are you doing here?" Thomas was surprised. "Drink?"

Walter shook his head no. "I'm on the job, Thomas."

"So is Grandfather."

They chuckled, then Thomas's grandfather announced, "I asked Walter to join us, because he has some very interesting news."

Walter had everyone's attention. He opened the folder and began reading. "Regarding the death of the priest, Father Liam O'Malley, recently some evidence came to light that has closed the case on Missing Person File No. 13595."

"What?" Macy was the first to respond, sitting forward and placing her martini on the coffee table. "What evidence? How do you know?"

"We conducted a private investigation and determined the case was closed due to the discovery of a confession in a safety deposit box in a Montreal bank. The box was opened after its owner died, the confession was found and then submitted to the local police. The owner, Mrs. Stella Good, stated that her husband, Mr. Robert Good, along with Mr. Frank Burns, killed the priest. Her husband, Mr. Good, was the cab-driver accomplice. He buried the priest's body under the new city hall in Ottawa after Mr. Burns was injured, apparently by a hit-and-run at the scene of the murder. Mr. Good and Mr. Burns were working on the orders of their local mob boss at the time. Her husband had confessed this to her as he was dying, and she wanted to let the priest's family know before the secret was lost forever."

Walter stopped reading and snapped the folder shut. "I suppose killing a priest makes you want to confess before you meet your maker." He cleared his throat then continued. "Incidentally, bones were found at that location several decades ago during construction, but they were never identified. In the 1950s Ottawa grew about five times its size. Bones were found at several sites, including the Mackenzie King Bridge, where the Department of National Defence is, and the 417 highway, so Father O'Malley sure wasn't the only one. Also, the hitman's brother, Charles Burns was a cop who was later involved in guarding a mob wise guy who turned informant. The guy died before trial. The whole Burns family was considered crooked."

No one spoke for a moment, then Vaughn and John grinned at each other. "Wait," John said. "The guy we ran over didn't die?" Walter shook his head and said, "No, sir. He was just injured."

"I guess we're not wanted men anymore," Vaughn said, then took another puff off his cigar.

"Guess not," John replied with a corresponding puff of his.

"Well, that calls for a toast." Thomas raised his glass and the others responded in kind. "To the best bingo bastards in town, free men at last!"

They all laughed. John drained his glass, motioned to Thomas for a refill, then said, "Now Thomas, if you'll excuse us, the rest of us have some business to attend to."

Macy put her glass down and stood, but he waved at her. "Where are you going, young lady? You stay put. My grandson can wait for you outside."

She looked at Thomas questioningly, but he only smiled as he handed the drink back to his grandfather. "Certainly. I'll be in the lobby," Thomas said to her, then left.

Thomas closed the office door behind him, said goodbye to Eleanor, then took the elevator to the lobby. Once there, he strolled back and forth in front of the large windows. After several minutes, he stood in front of the large directory on the wall beside the elevators. He was fairly certain his grandfather and Walter were offering Macy a job. He had spoken to them earlier about the entire endeavour and the part she had played in ending the blackmailing scheme. Over the course of the discussion, he had speculated what more she could have accomplished with access to better resources. It was only after a few interested questions from them that he clued in and suggested they talk to her about her ideas for security systems testing, which could be applied in various departments of the company in various ways. She'd be connected, to him and his family, in multiple ways. He liked that idea.

Eventually, the elevator dinged, the doors opened, and out strode Macy. Thomas had strolled back to the far end of the lobby again. As he turned towards her, she stopped in front of the directory. Given that her new position was to be kept confidential to allow her the anonymity the job required, her name would probably never appear on the board. That was okay. She turned to look at Thomas, and gave him a shit-eating grin.

December 14, 1952

Dear Diary,

As Mama says, it's best to start at the beginning. I have some catching up to do with you, so let me start back in the summer. Vaughn came home, and it was wonderful to have him back. He started visiting again of course, to see Bobby, but Bobby is … different. He's not the man he used to be, the war changed him. So Vaughn and I do most of the talking.

It was so nice to have another adult in the house who talks to me! Dinner time has become very quiet with just the two of us. Every now and then we have John and Barbara over, and Vaughn and whatever girl he brings, but John's quite busy with his business and it's usually just the three of us, Bobby, Vaughn and me.

I don't know how to say what I have to say next. One night, when it was just the three of us down at the tavern having a drink, Bobby got surly and left early. Vaughn and I were still having a good time though, listening to the band, so we stayed for another drink. Then he walked me home. He asked if I'm happy, because he's noticed the change in Bobby too. I could tell it took a lot for Vaughn to ask. The question startled me and I stopped right there in the middle of the sidewalk. Just like I did so many years ago.

I finally blurted it out to Vaughn that if I hadn't been such a silly girl I wouldn't have gotten us into all that trouble all those years ago. I was the one who wanted to see the priest, and I was the one who screamed, and I was the one who couldn't move since I was so scared. I just kept telling him I'm sorry.

He held my hands and pressed them to his chest. He said he was one who should be sorry, for taking a nice girl like me into a bar in the first place. He said he's been blaming himself the whole time. If he wasn't trying to impress me that night, none of this would have happened, and Bobby wouldn't have killed a man so young, then maybe he would be alright still, maybe he would've gotten through the war easier.

Vaughn said he saw a lot of young men kill and be killed in the war, and it made him realize how young and foolish we all were. He said he had many regrets. But we can't undo what we did, and we still can't go back to Ottawa, so he can't go home either.

I started crying. We hadn't talked about what happened in years. Vaughn wiped my tears away with his hand, then cupped my cheek and stared at me. He tilted my chin up and kissed me.

I feel wrong just writing this down, but Lord forgive me, it was wonderful.

We didn't say anything after that; he just walked me home, then he kissed me again at the door. I know I should worry about the neighbours but it didn't matter, nothing mattered, just Vaughn kissing me.

A week or two went by, and we pretended nothing had happened. But Bobby hurt his bad leg and had to go to the hospital for an operation. He was only in for one night, but Vaughn... That night...

Now I'm going to have a baby! I'm finally going to have my own family. I am so ashamed but I don't regret it. I have so many regrets to live with, but not this, not my baby.

AUTHOR'S EXPLANATION

The main event that starts our story, the priest's murder, is a version of reality. In 2005 I read an article entitled, "Note from the grave opens file on 66-year-old New York mystery" by Steven Edwards in the *Ottawa Citizen*. Judge Joseph Crater disappeared in 1930. He was last seen in a cab and despite years of searching, not a trace was found. It took a letter marked Do Not Open Until My Death to finish his story. It was written by the wife of one of the men involved in the judge's murder, who buried him under the Coney Island boardwalk, where the New York Aquarium now stands — and where skeletons were found during construction in the 1950s. To make Vaughn and his friends fit the appropriate ages, I moved the action up by twenty years and relocated it to Canada. All the other historical references are as they are described. It is true that many Canadian men served with the United States armed forces during the Korean War and that the Cold War started in Canada with a Russian clerk defecting.

And yes, Ottawa was the bingo capital of North America.

ACKNOWLEDGEMENTS

Special thanks to my editor, Alison Larabie Chase, to Donald Lanouette of Ottawa Brands for the cover design, and to the wonderful team at Iguana.